Lights, Camera, Rebecca!

A Rebecca Classic
Volume 2

by Jacqueline Dembar Greene

Am

Published by American Girl Publishing

Questions or comments? Call 1-800-845-0005, visit **americangirl.com**, or write to Customer Service, American Girl, 8400 Fairway Place, Middleton, WI 53562.

Printed in China
14 15 16 17 18 19 20 LEO 10 9 8 7 6 5 4 3 2 1

Cover image by Michael Dwornik and Juliana Kolesova

Cataloging-in-Publication Data available from the Library of Congress

To my father, George Dembar, and to Julie, Gloria,
Shirlee, and Jack for sharing their memories

To Monty, Laurie, Martha, and Jane,
who cheered me on even when the ride got bumpy

And to my husband, Mal, who shared
the kvetching and the kvelling

Beforever

Beforever is about making connections. It's about exploring the past, finding your place in the present, and thinking about the possibilities your future can bring. And it's about seeing the common thread that ties girls from all times together. The inspiring characters you will meet stand up for what they care about most: Helping others. Protecting the earth. Overcoming injustice. Through their courageous stories, discover how staying true to your own beliefs will help make your world better today—and tomorrow.

TABLE *of* CONTENTS

Max's Magic

CHAPTER 1

r. Goldberg cranked the handle on the phonograph in his candy shop, and the bright, tinkly sound of a piano filled the store. A singer's voice crooned,

Come on and hear, come on and hear
Alexander's Ragtime Band.
Come on and hear, come on and hear,
It's the best band in the land!

Rebecca hummed along, and her friend Rose snapped her fingers in time to the lively music.

"Isn't it swell to hear records?" Rebecca asked. "Just think—if we had a phonograph, we could play music whenever we wanted."

The tempo of the song slowed as the machine

wound down. Mr. Goldberg put on a new record and cranked the handle.

Rebecca headed toward the door. "We'd better go."

"Oh, not yet!" Rose protested. She clung to Rebecca's arm. "Let's hear the next song."

"I think we've hung around long enough without buying anything," Rebecca whispered. "I don't want to annoy Mr. Goldberg."

"I don't think he minds," Rose said. "It's awfully quiet in here for a Saturday afternoon." Only two customers sat on swiveling stools, sipping frothy egg creams. "Since this week is Passover, I guess hardly anybody is eating out." Rose looked longingly at jars filled with brightly colored jelly beans. "I sure would love a handful of those." She followed reluctantly as Rebecca held the door open.

"So would I," Rebecca said, "but Mama won't even let me order a soda. There are so many foods we can't eat during Passover, she and Bubbie don't trust anything they haven't made in their own kitchens."

The girls strolled up the street, enjoying the sunshine that warmed the spring afternoon. Rose shrugged. "Still, it's fun eating the special Passover foods we have only once a year, like *matzo*. Don't you think so?"

"Usually I do," Rebecca agreed. "Except for this year." She hesitated a moment. "Tomorrow's my birthday."

"Oooh—your birthday!" Rose exclaimed. "That is one of the best things in America. Back in Russia, my family never celebrated birthdays—not like here. Are you going to have a party?"

Rebecca scuffed her shoes along the sidewalk. "That's the problem—we've been so busy cleaning and cooking for Passover, I think everyone has forgotten." She kicked at a pebble and added glumly, "Anyway, I couldn't have a birthday cake unless it was as flat as matzo! What fun is a birthday without a big, fluffy cake?"

"Oh, Rebecca," Rose said, putting her arm around her friend, "how awful. No party, and no cake either. Well, if you're not having a party this year, then next year I think you should have two!"

Rebecca knew that her friend was trying to cheer her up. She forced a small smile.

"Let's walk the long way to your house and see

what's playing at the movie theater," Rose said. She steered Rebecca down a side street, whistling "Alexander's Ragtime Band" as she walked.

"What a boring day," Rebecca grumbled. "First we go to the candy store, where I can't even order a soda, and now to the movies, which my parents say I'm too young to see."

"It's fun looking at the posters, though," Rose said. "Don't you love seeing the beautiful actresses?"

The girls ducked around a gang of boys playing stickball and passed some girls playing jacks on the sidewalk. In a few more blocks, they came to the marble columns of the Orpheum Photo Play Theater. Giant letters blazed across the golden marquee: "Lillian Armstrong in *Cleopatra*."

Rebecca felt a cool rush of air as she and Rose stepped into the shade under the marquee. It gave Rebecca shivers to be so close to the theater. She still remembered the afternoon last fall when Max had brought the entire family to see a Charlie Chaplin movie. It was the first and only time her parents had let her attend. When the theater lights dimmed and the show began, Rebecca had felt an excitement like nothing before. It was astonishing to see pictures moving on a screen.

"Look at this!" Rose exclaimed. Rebecca gazed at the posters in gilded frames on either side of the entrance. A sultry actress with shadowed eyes outlined in black stared boldly out at them. Her straight hair was adorned with a golden headdress. She wore a low-cut dress and held an open-mouthed snake close to her chest.

"My family would especially never let me see this one!" Rebecca croaked. "It looks scary!"

"But it's about a real person," Rose said. "It's the story of Cleopatra, who was queen of Egypt. It's about history!"

"Try telling that to Bubbie," Rebecca muttered, imagining the stern look her grandmother would give her if she dared ask to see such a movie. "Maybe she'd let me go to the movies if they made one about the history of Passover, when the Jews escaped from slavery in Egypt." She pretended to be a barker calling people to the theater. She cupped her hands around her mouth and called in a husky voice, "See Moses lead his people to freedom! Watch as the Jews flee across the desert with nothing to eat but unleavened bread!"

"You know, that's not a bad idea," Rose remarked. "You should tell your cousin Max. Isn't he a movie actor?"

Rebecca nodded. "The best part would show how the Jews couldn't get across the Red Sea. The pharaoh's soldiers would be right behind them, and the Jews would be sure they're going to be captured. But Moses raises his staff, and the sea parts as the Jews rush across safely." She raised her arms in a sweeping gesture. "Let my people go!" she recited in a deep voice, as if she were playing the role of Moses.

"That would make a thrilling moving picture," Rose agreed, "as long as God parted the sea again for the filming."

"Come on," Rebecca said. "It's getting late."

But Rose lingered under the marquee, reading all the posters out loud. She pointed to the glamorous poster of Lillian Armstrong. "I don't think I've heard of this Cleopatra actress before."

"She must be new," said Rebecca. "I haven't seen her in a motion picture magazine. Of course, I only get to see the ones I can sneak away from my sisters."

The air was turning cooler. "We really should go," Rebecca insisted. At last, Rose headed back to the side-walk and ambled along toward Rebecca's row house, stopping to admire the window displays in the stores along the route. The girls paused at a tempting array of pastries and cakes in the window of an Italian bakery.

"You'd think that even at Passover, it would be okay to have a birthday cake," Rebecca blurted out. "I mean, Moses led the Jews out of Egypt thousands of years ago. We know they escaped without enough time to let their bread rise, and the unleavened bread was baked into flat matzos—but why do we have to worry about it today?"

"To remember how hard life was when the Jews were slaves," Rose said. "Eating matzos instead of bread and cake helps us remember our ancestors."

Rebecca felt a twinge of guilt. Mama and Bubbie had cooked for days to prepare the *seders,* the festive Passover meals they shared on the first two nights. The seders were feasts of delicious foods that followed a retelling of the Jews' journey out of Egypt to freedom. Passover was one of the most important Jewish holidays.

"It's probably wrong to even wish for a cake," Rebecca confessed. "I guess I just have to skip my birthday this year."

"Think about something fun," Rose suggested as they approached Rebecca's building. "I know—let's play hopscotch. Do you have any chalk?"

"I don't really feel like it," Rebecca said, heading up the front stoop.

"Well, let's just sit outside for a while, then," Rose said, plopping herself down on the top step.

"It's too chilly," Rebecca said, pulling Rose up.

Rose followed Rebecca into the kitchen, but the apartment was strangely quiet. "Oh, it's you, Rebecca! You're home already?" Mama asked, hastily throwing a napkin over a plate. "Everyone's out playing," Mama added before Rebecca had even asked. "I've got to take this upstairs to Bubbie." She picked up the covered dish and headed out the door.

"I'm hungry," Rebecca said when Mama had left. She looked in the icebox, but there was nothing except a jar of cold leftover soup. Rebecca sighed. She took a piece of matzo from a basket on the table and offered one to Rose. "Do you want jam on it?" she asked.

Rose shook her head. "I've got an idea—let's go up and give the pigeons a taste. I wonder if they like matzo."

Rebecca smiled at the thought. "Good idea!" She loved feeding the pigeons that the janitor kept in cages on the rooftop.

As the girls stepped into the hallway, Rebecca heard Bubbie calling from the top landing. "Rebecca! Come by me for a minute." Rebecca sighed. She couldn't think of any chores she might have forgotten. She peered up the stairwell.

"Come, *bubeleh*," her grandmother said, using her favorite Yiddish word for "sweetie." "I need some help."

Rebecca took a few steps up. "Can I come up later?" she called. "My friend Rose is here."

"So, you'll both come," Bubbie said. "Hurry, now." Rebecca climbed the stairs, her feet dragging. Rose followed a few steps behind her.

Bubbie smiled, her eyes crinkling at the corners as she nudged Rebecca inside. What was Bubbie so pleased about?

"Rose and I were—" Rebecca started to explain, but before she could finish, a chorus of voices shouted, "Surprise!"

From behind the furniture, Rebecca's friends Lucy, Gertie, and Sarah all jumped out, along with cousin Ana. Aunt Fannie and Uncle Jacob stepped from behind the bedroom door, laughing. Her cousins Josef and Michael called *"Mazel tov*—congratulations!" Mama and Papa and Rebecca's brothers and sisters were all crowded into the tiny apartment. Rebecca was speechless.

Mama gave her a hug. "Did you really think we'd forget your birthday?" she asked.

Rebecca felt giddy with pleasure. They hadn't forgotten after all. She grinned at Rose. "You knew about the party all along! That's why you kept thinking of excuses not to come back here."

"I could barely keep it secret!" Rose giggled. "You were so glum thinking you couldn't have a party because of Passover."

"What, you think we can't eat because of this holiday?" Bubbie said, passing around a plate of sweets. "Holidays are for eating—and so are birthdays!"

"And we're going to make egg creams for everyone," Papa announced. He held a blue glass bottle of seltzer, while Grandpa brought out a jar of homemade chocolate syrup.

There was a sharp knock on the door. *Rap-rap-a-tap-tap!* Rebecca knew the code. She ran to the door and gave two taps to complete the rhythm. *Rap-rap!* She pulled open the door, and sure enough, there was cousin Max.

"I hear there's a party with lots of food!" Max stepped into the crowded room. "Come with me, birthday girl," he said, leading Rebecca to a chair. He pulled a flowery scarf from his pocket and draped it around Rebecca's neck. Then he cocked his head to one side. "Hmmm . . . I don't think this is quite right for you," he decided. Making a fist with one hand, he pushed the scarf into it with the other. Everyone watched, mesmerized, as the scarf disappeared.

"It's magic!" Benny exclaimed, clapping his hands.

Max tapped his fist with one finger and slowly said, "Abracadabra!" With a dramatic flick, he opened his hand. The scarf was gone, and in its place there was a pink paper rose.

"Oooh!" cried the group. They gave Max a round of applause. He bowed, handing Rebecca the flower. She beamed at Max.

Max scratched his head. "I don't know. What good

is a rose without anyplace to put it? Hold on . . ."

He retrieved a large round box from the hallway, which he placed in Rebecca's lap. She pulled the lid off and lifted out a cream-colored hat with a huge brim decorated with flowers.

"Goodness gracious!" gasped Mama. She frowned at Max. "I think you've been around theater people too long. Rebecca's only turning ten, you know!"

Max ignored Mama's protest. He tucked the rose in with the other flowers and set the hat on Rebecca's head.

"Oh, Max," Rebecca sighed, "I feel just like a movie star!"

"We have a present for you, too," Sadie said, "although it's not nearly as dramatic as that hat." She handed Rebecca a small envelope. Inside was a colored postcard with a picture of Charlie Chaplin on it. On the back, her sisters had written, "This entitles Rebecca Rubin to one motion picture show, with an ice cream soda to follow."

Rebecca enfolded her sisters in one big hug. "Do you really mean it?"

"Now that you're ten," Sophie smiled, "we think

you're old enough to go to the pictures with us."

Rebecca opened the rest of her presents and thanked everyone. Then Max stood in front of her and arranged the hat brim at a stylish tilt. When he stepped aside, Rebecca peered from under the brim to see Mama holding a big birthday cake, covered in swirly white frosting. Ten candles glowed on top.

"Happy birthday to you," Max began singing, and everyone joined in.

"A cake!" Rebecca cried. She ought to make a wish, but what more could she wish for? She blew the candles out in one breath. "I didn't think there could be a birthday cake on Passover!"

"It's a sponge cake," Mama explained, "made with special matzo flour."

"But how did you get it to rise up so high and fluffy?" Rebecca asked.

"It's easy when you use twelve eggs!" Mama replied.

"Twelve eggs?" Rebecca repeated in disbelief.

"It's extravagant, I know," said Mama, "but it's not every day that your daughter turns ten."

Grandpa and Papa made fizzy egg creams in tall

glasses while Mama served the cake. Everyone ate and laughed. Too soon, the party was over, and people began to leave.

Gertie turned to Rebecca. "Wherever are you going to wear that hat? I don't think Miss Maloney will allow it at school."

"Since it's school vacation this week," Lucy pointed out, "she can wear it at home."

Max frowned. "You can't have a hat like this one and only wear it at home. This hat is meant to be seen." His face lit up. "I've got it! Wear it Monday when I go to work at the motion picture studio."

Rebecca was puzzled. "Why should I wear it when you're at work?" she asked.

"Because you'll be coming with me," Max said. "Movie people can truly appreciate a hat like this!"

Rebecca caught her breath. "Come with you to the picture studio? Will I get to see a movie being made?" She glanced at her sisters. Sadie and Sophie looked positively green with jealousy.

Bubbie cleared her throat. "Just because there is no school doesn't mean pitcher-making place is for a respectable young lady to go. And in such a hat!"

All eyes turned to Max. "I beg to differ, my dear woman," he said with dignity. "All the actresses at the studio are respectable ladies."

"I don't think we should encourage this moving picture nonsense," Papa said.

Bubbie put her hands on her hips. "And *what* she will eat for lunch?"

Grandpa chimed in. "Monday is school vacation, maybe, but is still Passover. Moving-pitcher place doesn't have Passover food."

Rebecca didn't dare argue with Bubbie and Grandpa and Papa, especially in front of everyone. She looked at Mama and pleaded with her eyes.

Mama hesitated a moment and then put her hand on Papa's shoulder. Rebecca held her breath. "I could boil a couple of eggs and give her a banana and some leftover party cookies. And of course"—Rebecca joined in for the last item—"matzo!" she and Mama said in unison.

Mama smiled. "I think it will be all right for her to go with Max just this once. After all, she's not going to turn into an actress just because she visits a movie studio."

A New World

CHAPTER 2

n Monday morning, before anyone else in the household was awake, Rebecca was washed and dressed. She gave her hair one hundred brushstrokes and put on Max's birthday hat, admiring the way the brim framed her face with graceful curves. She quickly ate breakfast and then brushed her teeth until they glistened. After all, today she was going to meet movie actresses, so she wanted to look her very best.

Mama came into the kitchen and set about making lunches for Rebecca and for Papa to take with him to work. When Max bounded up the stairs, Rebecca was ready and waiting, her lunch box in her hand.

Max chattered on about the studio as they hopped onto the speedy subway. Rebecca had heard about the underground trains but never thought she'd be riding in one, zooming under the streets of New York. When it screeched to a stop, she and Max emerged into the sunlight across from the ferry landing.

"Here's our merry band!" Max exclaimed, joining a boisterous group already seated on the boat. Max introduced Rebecca to some of the actors and crew. The actresses wore stylish dresses and hats and had applied lip color and rouge. The actors wore smart suits and jaunty straw hats with colorful hatbands. They all talked about the scenes to be filmed that day, using language Rebecca had never heard before. Her ears perked up as she tried to guess the meaning of "fades," "takes," and "glass plates." She was pretty sure that a glass plate wasn't something to eat from.

As the ferry glided out into the harbor, Rebecca looked back at the skyline. This was the first time she had ever left the city.

The tall buildings that people called skyscrapers loomed above Manhattan. Rebecca had to agree that they truly seemed to scrape the sky. When the boat sailed past the Statue of Liberty, she raced to the railing to gaze at it. The statue's torch glinted against the blue sky.

Rebecca knew that a young Jewish woman had written the poem inscribed on the statue's base. Rebecca had learned the poem in school, and she especially loved the lines that welcomed immigrants like her parents and grandparents to America. "'Give me your tired, your poor, your huddled masses yearning to breathe free,'" she murmured, quoting the poem.

As Rebecca went back to her seat, she noticed a young couple sitting together near the back of the boat. The woman's hat sprouted a single white feather that arched over her head and nestled next to her cheek. She was quite dainty, with a delicate build and the slimmest waist Rebecca had ever seen. But her hair was the most startling thing about her. It wasn't the color, which was a modest brown—it was the length. Under her fitted hat, the woman's hair was cropped short. Bubbie had been worried about the actresses not being "ladies." She would think it perfectly scandalous to see a young woman with her hair bobbed!

Rebecca couldn't stop staring, but the woman was too absorbed in conversation to notice. "See that lady with her hair cut short?" Rebecca whispered to Max. "She looks familiar somehow, but I don't know why."

Max fidgeted with his bow tie. "Ah, yes," he said, "that's our leading lady, the studio's newest shining star, Miss Lillian Armstrong."

"She's Cleopatra!" Rebecca exclaimed. "I saw her on a movie poster at the Orpheum! Her name is on the marquee."

"I'm lucky just to have my name listed in the film credits," Max muttered. "But definitely below hers. I'm not in the same heavenly constellation as Lillian Armstrong. At least, not yet." He looked at the chatting couple. "That swell beside her is none other than Don Herringbone, veteran of stage and screen." The man was short, but he had a lofty manner about him.

Rebecca giggled. "What a funny name—herring bone. I've never seen one in a moving picture, but I see them all the time in jars of pickled fish!"

"'Don Juan' is what I call him," Max said in a low voice. "That's the name of a famous character in a book who always has a different sweetheart. Too bad Lillian doesn't realize she's just part of the adoring crowd to Don Juan."

The ferry horn blew two loud blasts and chugged toward the landing in New Jersey. A deckhand secured the boat and lowered a gangplank to the wooden dock.

"There's our ride," Max said, pointing to a motor bus idling on the road.

"A subway ride, then the ferry, and now a motor bus," Rebecca said with delight. "And all on my very first trip away from home." It was going to be a day filled with firsts. "I'm going to remember this forever."

"I still remember my journey from Russia to America as if it were yesterday," Max said. "But for me, it was an oxcart from town, then steerage on a ship, and finally the ferry to Manhattan. I thought I had landed in another world."

Rebecca and Max settled onto a stiff bench seat, while the idling motor bus rattled and sputtered. Don Herringbone guided Lillian Armstrong to the back, his hand under her elbow.

"Good morning, ladies and gentlemen," called the bus driver. "Hold on to your hats, and we're off!"

Rebecca reached up and held fast to her new hat, causing chuckles around her. She laughed at her mistake, realizing the bus driver's comment had just been a joke. As the bus bounced along, Rebecca's hat stayed firmly on her head.

"Oooh!" she squealed, as the bus picked up speed.

"Take this little lady to Coney Island," a square-jawed actor advised Max. "She's a natural for the roller coaster!"

Rebecca watched the sunlit roadside speeding by outside the window. They passed a few horse-drawn wagons, but there were no pushcarts, or crowds of shoppers, or kids playing stickball. Instead, Rebecca saw thick stands of trees, and small towns and farm fields appeared and quickly disappeared behind the rumbling bus. There was not a single apartment building nor more than a few stores scattered along the way. Where would you buy pickles and herring? Where was the candy store? It seemed to Rebecca that she was rushing away from everything she knew—almost as if she herself were an immigrant, leaving her old country behind and looking for opportunity in a new and unfamiliar world.

The bus rounded a curve, bumped along a rutted dirt road, and came to a stop in front of a tall iron fence. Molded into the iron gate were the words "Banbury Cross Studios."

"Why, the studio's name is like the Mother Goose

rhyme," said Rebecca. "'Ride a cockhorse to Banbury Cross, to see a fine lady upon a white horse.'"

"You never know what you'll see roaming across the studio lot," Max told her, "and a white horse isn't out of the question."

A security guard swung the wide gates open. The bus lumbered along past a series of warehouses and parked in front of a long, wood-shingled building.

"Whoopee!" exclaimed one of the actresses as she stepped off the bus. "Today the director is going to notice me. I feel it in my bones." She waved her ostrich-plumed hat in the air. "L.B., here I come!"

Rebecca tugged at Max's sleeve. "Who's L.B.?"

"None other than the Grand Pooh-Bah himself, Lawrence B. Diamond, director extraordinaire," Max said as he ushered Rebecca into the building's expansive entryway. "When you see him in the studio, you will know instantly who he is."

Corridors led off in three directions. "The dressing rooms are down there," Max pointed. He turned. "Film studios are that-a-way."

Rebecca looked toward the third corridor. "What's down there?" she asked.

"No place we're supposed to be," said Max, "unless nobody sees us." He tiptoed to the entrance and peered down the dark hallway. He motioned to Rebecca, and she imitated him, creeping up behind him as if they were sneaking up on a sleeping giant. "Let's investigate," Max intoned, and Rebecca followed him gamely, tiptoeing all the way.

Max looked up and down the empty corridor, then opened a door labeled Property Room. He whisked Rebecca inside. "Sometimes we're outdoors on location, with real trees and roads and gardens, but most of the time we're indoors and need lots of props to shoot the scene."

"Shoot?" Rebecca repeated. "You use guns?"

"Oh, no," Max laughed. "When the cameraman starts rolling the camera, we call it *shooting.*"

Rebecca thought it seemed odd to roll a camera, but not nearly as odd as the room she found herself in. Shelves holding lamps, flowerpots, dishes, glasses, and linens lined the walls. Hat racks, chairs, sofas, and iceboxes were jumbled in every available space. A rickety table held three phonographs, their shiny horns facing different directions. Wooden crates held swords and rifles, and a dummy dressed in a three-piece suit slumped in a corner.

"All this flotsam and jetsam are the props we use in stage sets," Max explained. "And that's Harry," he added, pointing to the dummy. "He's fallen off more cliffs than any other actor, and he never complains."

Rebecca smiled. "He does look rather lonely, though." She walked over to where the mannequin sat and shook his limp hand. "How do you do, Harry?" she said politely. "It's so thrilling for me to meet a real picture star!"

Max grinned. "You've definitely made Harry the happiest movie actor around. He gets even less respect for what he does than the rest of us."

"But everyone loves motion pictures," Rebecca said. "Except for my parents and Bubbie and Grandpa, that is." She looked sheepishly at Max.

"People don't understand what we do," Max said. "They think we just clown around and don't lead respectable lives with a settled home and a steady job."

Max's life was certainly different from her family's, but Rebecca thought it was more exciting, too.

Max pointed to a pile of large gray rocks in a corner.

"Could you toss me one of those boulders? That big one there will do nicely for today's shoot."

Rebecca wanted to help in any way she could, but she didn't think she could lift the heavy rock in front of her. "Gosh, Max, I don't know," she said.

"Go on," Max said. "Everyone around here has to do her share."

Taking a deep breath, Rebecca put her arms around the rock. It felt rough and rather scratchy. She began lifting slowly. Why, it didn't weigh more than an ounce! In fact, it felt hollow inside. She stood up, holding it awkwardly.

"Papier-mâché!" Max grinned. "We've got mountains of 'em."

Rebecca threw the rock to Max. "Catch!" she yelled as the boulder whizzed through the air. Max's arms flailed out wildly. He barely caught the rock as it sailed toward his head.

"I guess I deserved that," he laughed, dropping the fake boulder back onto the pile. He led Rebecca out, closing the door behind them.

"Who's the doll-baby in the scrumptious hat?" said a sweet voice. An actress was walking up the hallway, carrying a brown wig with flowing ringlets.

"This is my cousin, Rebecca Rubin," Max said. "Rebecca, meet Miss Lillian Armstrong."

Rebecca smiled shyly and found she could barely speak. "Glad to meet you," she managed. Wait until she told Rose that she had met Cleopatra herself!

"I saw you on the bus this morning, didn't I?" Miss Armstrong asked. "Say, how would you like to see me turn from a real girl into a movie actress?"

Rebecca nodded, unable to say a word.

"I'll take this doll-baby with me," Miss Armstrong said to Max. "You need to get ready for the shoot. You know how L.B. feels about actors being punctual."

Max bent down a little and whispered loudly in Rebecca's ear, "Don't let her steal that hat of yours!" With a wink and a wave, he strolled off down the corridor, whistling brightly.

Miss Armstrong opened her dressing room door. Painted on the outside was a shiny gold star with her name in black lettering just underneath. Rebecca wondered if Max had a star painted on his door, too. Inside the small room, the wallpaper was printed with white lilies, and a vase of fresh lilies perched on the corner of the dressing table. A full-length triple mirror stood in one corner of the room, and an oval mirror with round lights sat on the dressing table. Everywhere she looked, Rebecca saw her own reflection. She couldn't help admiring the effect of her new hat.

"First of all, you must call me Lily," said the actress. "We aren't very formal here." She pointed to an upholstered chaise longue. "Make yourself comfortable." Lily placed the wig on top of a coat tree and kicked off her shoes. She stepped behind a Chinese folding screen and tossed her clothes across the top. A moment later, Lily emerged wearing a long, flowered robe and settled gracefully on a stool at her dressing table. She opened a small case and lined up a row of jars and foil-covered sticks. "My precious greasepaint box," Lily explained. "Without it, I wouldn't have a movie face."

Lily smoothed on cold cream, then squeezed a bit of buff-colored cream from a tube and covered her face until it looked ghostly pale. Next she drew thick black lines around her eyes and brushed inky paste onto her eyelashes. With her pinky finger, she rubbed on ruddy brownish lip color. Finally, she dusted on a coating of powder and patted it down with a soft rabbit's foot.

"Why do you have to wear all that makeup?" Rebecca asked politely.

"Without it, my face would photograph as a dark shadow. And after I make my skin so pale, I've got to darken around my eyes, or they wouldn't show up at all." Lily seemed to know that the makeup made her look rather ghoulish. She made a witchy cackle and clawed at the air with her fingers. "Now I've got you in my clutches!" she teased. Rebecca gave a mock scream and shrank back, giggling.

"I know I look odd," Lily admitted, "but it all comes out bright and natural on film." She turned to the mirror again and wrapped a thin scarf around her head. "And this hair bob is perfect for me—so much easier to tuck under a wig." She waved her arm dramatically. "And, doll-baby, I'm always in a wig!"

So there was a reason for the actress's short hair. How could Bubbie argue with that?

A light knock sounded on the door. *"Entrez!"* Lily called. A plump woman came in with an evening gown draped over her arm.

"My dress!" Lily exclaimed. "Mabel, you're a wonder." To Rebecca she said, "I think Mabel could fit an elephant and then remake the dress for a mouse!"

"And in this case, you're the mouse," the dress-maker said, smiling. "It's all nipped in around the waist now." Lily dropped her dressing robe on the floor and held her arms straight up in the air. Mabel pulled the dress over the actress's head. It swished down around Lily's dainty ankles, and Mabel began looping tiny buttons at the back. She pulled and smoothed at the fabric until it hung perfectly.

"Now for your hair," Mabel said. Lily sat down as Mabel fitted the wig onto Lily's head. In spite of the strange makeup, she looked stunning.

"You look like a painting," Rebecca murmured in admiration.

Lily smiled, her teeth pearly white behind the dark lip paint. "I'm playing the daughter of a wealthy society family," she said. "We are about to host a swell social affair. Of course, we'll start with cocktails on the lawn."

Mabel laughed. "That depends on whether or not the set designers painted you a lawn!"

Lily strapped on a pair of delicate shoes that were more elegant than any in Papa's shoe store. Mabel picked up the clothes Lily had left strewn about. She clucked her disapproval, just as Bubbie would have, but Lily didn't seem to notice.

"Shall we?" Lily asked, offering her arm to Rebecca. Together they walked toward the set.

"What else happens in the scene?" Rebecca asked.

"Well, my parents have chosen a rich man for me to marry, but I don't like him." She stamped her tiny foot and frowned until her dark penciled eyebrows nearly touched. "He's vile! I would rather die than marry such a cad!" She changed her expression to a dreamy look and sighed deeply. "I'm secretly in love with the gardener. Of course, my parents wouldn't ever approve, and there's the plot."

Rebecca thought the story sounded a lot like real life. In fact, it sounded a bit like her own life. *Only in my case,* she realized, *it's movies I'm in love with—and my parents would never approve!*

Lily pushed open heavy double doors, and Rebecca entered a huge room with a glass ceiling. Light flooded across a stone patio with a carved railing and two stately urns overflowing with paper flowers. Behind the patio, the front of a mansion was painted on a large canvas backdrop. The mansion looked so real, Rebecca almost believed she could step inside. But the workings of the movie studio intruded into the illusion with wires, machines, and rows of spotlights. Cameras with round lenses were perched on tall tripods that looked as if they might walk across the floor on their own.

"Well, doll-baby, this is it," Lily said, waving her arm expansively.

"I never heard of a ceiling made of glass," Rebecca marveled.

"It gives us lots of natural light, and we don't have to worry about the weather," Lily told her.

A burly man with a bushy red mustache ambled up to them. "And if it's dark, we've got electric lights. Being inside gives us more days of shooting," he said, "and it keeps the sets steady. Even a light breeze can make the canvas backdrops sway, and then the film looks fuzzy."

"This is Roddy Fitzgerald," Lily said, "our chief carpenter."

"A carpenter to make moving pictures?" Rebecca asked, looking up at him in surprise.

"Sure—and who else would build the stage platforms?" Roddy replied in a lilting Irish brogue. "I also build stairs, walls, balconies, and the frames for the backdrops." He arched his thick eyebrows. "You didn't think the scenery in moving pictures was real, did you now?"

"It must be swell to be the carpenter for a motion-picture studio," Rebecca said.

"Well, it surely is different," Roddy said. "You build something and then chop it up a month later. We don't save sets because of the danger of fires. You've heard of Thomas Edison, I suppose? His moving picture studio was just down the road here, but it burned to the ground around Christmas. You can't be too careful." Roddy sighed. "I'd like to have my own business someday, and build things to last. Now, that would be grand."

Rebecca nodded, but she didn't really understand. How could working anywhere else in the world be better than here?

Don Herringbone entered the studio, his face covered with pasty makeup and his eyebrows darkened, giving him a menacing look.

"There's my wicked suitor," Lily laughed.

A curling mustache was pasted on Don Herringbone's

upper lip, and he was dressed in a tuxedo with a silk cravat at his neck. His hair was slicked down with shiny brilliantine. Rebecca thought he looked a bit oily.

"Lillian, my dear," he said. He took her hand and lightly kissed it. "You know you're in love with me!" Lily drew back coyly, her head turned to one side. Rebecca was fascinated. Was this part of their act?

Just then, Max walked over. He wore rough tweed pants with suspenders buttoned over a loose white shirt, open at the neck. His hair fell in tousled waves under a soft cap, and his face was the same ghostly pale as the other players'.

"Ah, the gardener," Mr. Herringbone drawled, sounding haughty.

"Beware this scoundrel in fancy clothes," Max advised Lillian.

Rebecca felt a shiver of delight. Were they all acting? Why, acting for a movie didn't seem any different from playing with her friends and just pretending. Rebecca could playact, too. She gestured toward Lily with a flick of her hand and spoke in a high voice. "I'm sure such an elegant lady knows her best suitor."

"You bet I do, doll-baby," Lillian laughed.

Max coughed a little. "Come on, Rebecca," he said, steering her away from the group. "Let's find a good spot where you can sit and watch."

At one side of the room, the actresses and actors who had been on the ferry leaned against walls, sat on chairs, and perched on props. "Welcome to the garden," said an actress in a feathered hat. Rebecca recognized the ostrich plumes. This was the young woman who had been so certain that she would land a role today. "In case you can't tell," the actress said, "we're all lowly worms, just waiting to be dug up. Extras like us just wriggle around, hoping the Grand Pooh-Bah will pick us for a scene—any scene, just so we can pay the rent! Otherwise, it's move back in with Mama." The other extras groaned.

Another young actress glared at Rebecca. Her lips were painted fire-engine red, and her glossy nails were long and tapered. "Are you competition, or just visiting?"

"I'm just here to watch," Rebecca assured her, sitting on a hard wooden chair with her lunch box in her lap. "I'm not an actress."

"Bet you'd like to be, though," the actress replied. Rebecca squirmed under her steady gaze. How had she guessed what Rebecca was thinking? The actress turned to the other extras. "Watch out for this one," she warned, pointing a long-nailed finger at Rebecca.

Rebecca protested. "Oh no, my family would never—"

"You'll have to be as quiet as a sleeping mouse," Max cautioned her. "L.B. has a temper, and if you cause any trouble, he'll send you out."

Rebecca nodded gravely. "I won't even breathe loudly," she promised. She gave Max's hand a squeeze. "You look really handsome," she whispered. "Lots better than Don Juan. In fact, you're the best-looking ghost I've ever seen!" Max straightened up and strode off with a swagger in his step.

Kidlet on the Set

CHAPTER 3

A deep voice boomed across the studio. "Attention, please!"

Rebecca froze.

Stagehands, actors, and extras scampered toward a tall, lanky man holding a megaphone. His slim britches were tucked into a pair of tight boots, and he held a short leather stick. He looked like a magazine photo Rebecca had seen of an actor on horseback, but she guessed he was no actor, and no rider, either. He must be Lawrence B. Diamond, the director.

"We'll start from where we cut yesterday," he announced. "Diana," he said, gesturing to Lillian Armstrong, "find your mark!" Lily sauntered onto the patio set and stood precisely in one fixed spot at the rail. "Gus the gardener stands before her, holding up the flower," the director continued. A young man in a faded blue smock handed Max a white rose as he walked to the opposite side of the railing. Was it a real flower, or just paper?

"The villainous Rex Wentworth is spying on the young lovers," L.B. called out. Don Herringbone hunched behind a potted bush and peered out at the couple. Rebecca saw a chalked line on the floor that snaked around the patio. She could only imagine what Mama would say if Rebecca drew on the floor!

"When the camera rolls," L.B. called through his megaphone, "Gus hands Diana the rose. She breathes in its perfume and holds it against her heart. Gus points down the pathway, inviting Diana to join him. Diana, you look back nervously at the mansion. Are your parents watching? Your father would be furious if you considered marrying a man of such humble means. He might even disown you, and you would be penniless! But Gus's entreaties win you over. You step down the stairs and take his outstretched hand."

Rebecca was enthralled with the director's scenario. Max and Lily had to show the emotions their characters felt and act out a story. And they had to do it all without saying a word, because movies were silent.

Their acting had to be perfect.

"As the young lovers disappear down the path, holding hands, Rex Wentworth scowls and strokes his mustache. He will not lose Diana to this lowly gardener! His crafty eyes narrow as he thinks of a plan to foil the lovers. He slinks toward the mansion to inform Diana's parents about their daughter and the gardener—and win Diana for his own!"

L.B. began pacing in front of the set. "We need more action. More drama." He tapped his riding crop against the megaphone, and the noise echoed across the silent studio. Then he hit the megaphone with a resounding whack! Rebecca flinched.

"I've got it!" he shouted. "Diana has a little sister who sees everything. She runs off to warn the couple as soon as Rex leaves." He lifted his arms in frustration. "We need a kidlet!" he wailed. "Where am I going to get a kidlet now?"

The young actress in the feathered hat rushed forward, the plumes bobbing. "I've played kid roles before," she said eagerly. "You always say I've got a girlish look." She tilted her head and propped a finger against her chin.

L.B. considered, squinting at her in the bright light. Then he shook his head. "Not for this role, Bess." The actress walked off, her eyes downcast.

Rebecca had promised Max that she wouldn't make a peep, but in the blink of an eye, everything had changed. Here was a chance to step from her ordinary life into a thrilling new world. If she thought about it too long, she would miss her chance forever.

She jumped up from her seat. "I can do it," she announced. All the extras turned to stare.

"I knew it," said the young woman with the long, shiny nails. "Another scene stealer."

"Who are you, and what are you doing on my set?" thundered L.B. At that moment, Rebecca knew why the actors called him the Grand Pooh-Bah. Her knees felt as wobbly as Mama's noodles.

Max rushed to Rebecca's side. "It just so happens I've brought the perfect little sister along," he said. He draped his arm around her shoulder, bolstering her confidence. Rebecca tried to stand tall.

The director summoned Rebecca with a beckoning finger. The extras around her moved aside in two waves. To Rebecca it felt as if the Red Sea had parted once again, and she had to get across before it was too late. She stepped forward under L.B.'s steady gaze.

"Ever acted in a stage play?" he demanded.

If I admit the truth, he probably won't even consider putting me in the movie, she thought. But she couldn't lie. "No, sir," she gulped.

"Good!" L.B. declared. "Stage actors make lousy motion picture actors. All they want is applause ringing in their ears." He motioned Rebecca closer, and she took a few more halting steps. L.B. lifted her chin in his hand and turned her face to the right and then to the left. "Ummm," he said. "Great big eyes hiding under that spectacular hat." Now Rebecca smiled. "Aaah! Nice bright teeth!"

"She's not playing the Big Bad Wolf," Max said. "Just put a dress on her and roll 'em."

"Wardrobe!" L.B. shouted, and Mabel rushed up. "Something fancy," he ordered, "to go with this fabulous hat. And make it snappy! We've got a garden party to attend."

Mabel took Rebecca's hand and hurried her into a room filled with racks of clothes and a sewing machine. A round platform surrounded by mirrors stood at one end. It was just like one in the tailor's shop where Papa had his pants measured.

"There's got to be something here we can use," Mabel fussed. She waved her hand toward the racks of suits and elegant dresses.

"Did you make all these?" Rebecca wondered aloud.

"I do most of the women's clothes," Mabel said. "But some things, like this cape, are bought in used clothing shops." She draped a rippling fur-trimmed cape around Rebecca's shoulders before whisking it back to the rack. "This definitely won't do for a garden party." She rifled through the racks and pulled out a silky pink gown with a softly ruffled neckline.

With Mabel's help, Rebecca stepped out of her everyday clothes and into the shimmering gown. Mabel pulled the waist tighter and looked at the effect. With a pincushion in her hand, she led Rebecca to the round platform, quickly pinned the waist, and then sewed it quickly with wide, looping stitches.

Mabel pointed to a table with a makeup kit on it. "Let's get started on your face paint." Rebecca carefully set her hat on a chair while Mabel opened a jar of cold cream. She dabbed some lightly on Rebecca's face. Then she applied pale greasepaint and drew black liner around Rebecca's eyes.

"I look like a white-faced raccoon!" Rebecca sputtered.

"Don't jiggle!" Mabel scolded. "Pucker your lips as if you were going to give me a big kiss." Rebecca puckered, and Mabel painted on lip color with a tickly soft brush. Then she fluffed Rebecca's hair. "Look at all these lovely waves. I think we can almost match Miss Armstrong's curly wig," she said. She wet a comb and pulled it through Rebecca's hair, forming springy finger curls as she went.

Finally, Mabel fitted Rebecca's hat back on carefully. "At least you arrived with *some* of your costume," she smiled.

"It was a birthday present from Max," Rebecca said. "He thought movie people would truly appreciate it."

Mabel blushed a little. "That Max sure is a charmer, ain't he?" She fluffed out Rebecca's ringlets. "There now, you're ready to go."

Rebecca stood as still as a statue, staring at herself in the mirror. Was she really still Rebecca, or had she been transformed into a totally different girl?

There was no time to linger. Mabel handed Rebecca a frilly parasol and rushed her back to the set. The actors were lounging against the patio railing, and the cameraman was aiming his lens at the scene. "Light's perfect," he said, turning to the director. "Let's shoot."

"Ahh, here's our little miss," L.B. said, taking Rebecca's hand and leading her toward a vine-covered archway that stood just to the side of the patio. He pointed to a chalked X on the floor. "Stand on this mark," L.B. told her. "Then step under the archway. You look over and see Diana and Gus making goo-goo eyes at each other. You spy on them, and flash one of your brilliant smiles. Then you hear a sound." The director looked at her steadily. "How will the audience know you hear something?" he asked, and then he answered his own question. "You have to exaggerate every expression. Don't worry about overdoing it. Put your hand to your ear and cock your head as if you're straining to hear a sound. Then shrink back under the archway, look toward Rex, and open your eyes wide with fear! Next, crouch down and wait. When the others have gone, dash through the archway and run down the path after your sister."

Rebecca felt paler than the makeup on her face. Could she do what the director asked? There was so much to remember. At home, she had made up dozens of roles to pretend she was someone else, but this was different—this was a real moving picture!

"Let's rehearse it once without the camera," the director said as the other actors took their places on the set.

Rebecca began to go through the motions that L.B. had described. But as soon as she stepped toward the archway, he interrupted. "Watch those chalk marks! Anything outside the lines is out of the camera range. Start again," he ordered.

So that's what the chalk lines are for, Rebecca thought as she stepped onto the X and repeated the motions.

The director stopped her again. "Move more slowly, or the film will be blurry. Every motion comes out faster when we film it."

Rebecca tried again, slowing her movements. When she looked at Max and Lily, she told herself that these were not the people she knew, but her sister Diana and Gus the gardener. She smiled.

"Bigger smile! Let's see those pearly white teeth!"

the director shouted through his megaphone, his commands echoing through the studio.

Rebecca couldn't believe how hard it was to smile on demand. She knew she should be bubbling with happiness, but the smile felt false.

"Stop!" L.B. yelled. He strode over to Rebecca and bent down until they were eye to eye. Rebecca felt sure he was going to replace her with an experienced actress. She would have to step out of the dress and become a silent bystander again. But instead of sending her away, L.B. spoke to her kindly. "Got the jitters?" he asked.

Rebecca nodded. "I—I want to do it, but I don't know if I can."

"Pretend there's not another soul on this set except your sister and her beau," L.B. advised her.

Rebecca took a deep breath and went back to her mark. Papa thought actors were lazy, but acting in a movie was hard work. Rebecca tried to forget about everything except the story as she played the scene. She exaggerated every move, remembered to stay inside the chalk lines, and at the end ran *slowly* down the path.

"You've got it!" L.B. boomed through his megaphone. "Places, everyone!" Actors froze on their marks. The cameraman turned his cap so that the visor was facing backward and put his eye close to the camera.

The director raised his megaphone and tapped it with his riding crop. "And roll!" he yelled.

Faintly, Rebecca heard the ratcheting of a crank as the cameraman turned a handle. She shut out every sound except L.B.'s shouted instructions. Suddenly, it was easy to imagine she was at a fancy garden party, about to save her sister from a nasty suitor. She forgot about being Rebecca and became the role she played, going through the motions as if she were inside the body of another girl.

"And cut!" shouted L.B. "It's a take!" He turned to the cameraman. "Get this footage developed double-quick. I want to see it today."

Rebecca awoke as if from a dream. Had she really filmed a scene in a movie?

Max put his arm around her. "A natural!" he exulted.

"Not bad for a rookie," Lily said with a warm smile.

"Talented little kidlet," L.B. remarked as he headed off the set. "See you at lunch."

Music Wherever She Goes

CHAPTER 4

Still in their elegant gowns and greasepaint, Rebecca and Lily joined the rest of the crew for lunch. Their face makeup made them look chalky white, but they rubbed off the lip color so that they could eat lunch and not lip rouge. Max waved Rebecca over to where he stood in the cafeteria line.

"Gosh, Max," Rebecca fretted beside him. "Am I the only one bringing my lunch from home?"

Lily held up a small basket with a napkin folded on top. "You're going to have plenty of company today," she pointed out. "Lots of us aren't eating from the studio kitchen this week." Rebecca looked around and saw that several people were opening boxes and baskets and taking out homemade lunches.

As the cafeteria line moved forward, Lily looked

at Max with surprise. "Did you know the stew they're serving today has dumplings on top?" she asked. Dumplings were made with flour and leavening, and Max surely knew they were forbidden during Passover.

Max shrugged, looking sheepish. "Of course I wasn't going to eat the dumplings. But I don't have anything else."

"Come on, you can have some of my lunch," Rebecca offered, taking his hand. "Mama always gives me more than I can eat."

As they followed Lily to a table, Don Herringbone sauntered up, his painted eyebrows making him look threatening. "Come, Lily, my dear," he said, "we'll find a private table."

"Not today," the actress answered. "I'm keeping the kidlet company."

Mr. Herringbone looked insulted. "Well! That's a fine how-de-do," he sputtered. In a quick change of mood, he pasted on a charming smile and joined two extras nearby. The actresses gazed at him adoringly.

Max pulled out a chair for Lily and then for Rebecca before sitting down next to Roddy. The carpenter unwrapped a gigantic sandwich with meat and cheese hanging out the sides.

"Meet my companion, the leftover Easter ham," Roddy said, holding up his sandwich. "I'll be keepin' it company for days to come."

Max opened Rebecca's lunch box and rummaged around. "So, what have you got?" he asked. "Are you sure there's enough for me?"

"I've got plenty for both of us," said Roddy, offering half of his bulging sandwich. Max started to reach for it, but then with a guilty glance at Rebecca and Lily he quickly declined.

"Max!" Rebecca exclaimed. "You wouldn't really eat a sandwich on Passover, would you? Especially one with ham!" Jewish people never ate pork products, whether it was Passover or not. It just wasn't *kosher.*

Max's cheeks turned red, even through his heavy makeup. It was the first time Rebecca had ever seen him look embarrassed.

"Poor Max," Lily crooned. "Don't you have anyone to cook for you?" She opened her basket. "I've got enough to share." Lily took out small glass containers of herring salad, Russian beet and potato salad, and orange sections. Rebecca began to spread out her lunch on the table, as well. Just as she unwrapped her matzo, she saw Lily take some from her basket.

Rebecca grinned. "You have matzo, too!"

Lily nodded toward L.B. "Take a gander at the Grand Pooh-Bah himself." The director was munching on squares of matzo spread with jam.

Max took a bite of Lily's herring salad. "Delicious," he murmured.

Lily gave Max a warm smile. "At Passover, I pull out all my mother's recipes. She might not like my job, but she can't criticize my cooking."

Rebecca expected Max to offer a joking response, but instead, silence fell over the table. Max was so quiet when Lily was around, thought Rebecca. He definitely wasn't himself.

Roddy stood up. "I think we need to liven this place up a bit," he announced. A phonograph sat on an empty table, with a stack of records piled next to it. Roddy cranked the handle, and a scratchy voice sang from the speaker, "Down by the old mill stream, where I first met you . . ."

Max reached for Rebecca's hand and made a gentlemanly bow. "Shall we dance, *mademoiselle*?"

Here was the Max that Rebecca knew—always full of delightful surprises. She took his hand and struggled to follow his graceful box step. Soon the music led her along, and they swirled between the tables. Rebecca's fancy party gown swished with every turn.

"So," Max said as they glided along, "how do you like being an actress?"

"It's wonderful," Rebecca sighed. "I forgot I was me when I started acting. It seemed as if I actually became someone else. It's such fun pretending to be a different girl leading a completely different life!"

"Acting lets you shed your everyday skin and try on a new one," Max said. "There aren't many chances in life to do that." He twirled her around as the song ended. Roddy replaced the record with a ragtime piano tune.

"It's Scott Joplin!" Max exclaimed. "Let's keep dancing."

But Rebecca thought she had a better idea. "I've got to catch my breath," she fibbed, pulling Max to the table. "Why don't you dance with Lily?"

"Why, Max, I thought you'd never ask," Lily said

gaily. Max stood silently, as if he were rooted to the floor. With a private wink at Rebecca, Lily took Max's hand and led him away from the crowded tables. Rebecca nibbled her lunch and watched as Max swung Lily around the floor to the fast-paced music. Max was a smooth dancer, and Lily kept up with every move. When the record ended, they flopped down on their chairs, laughing.

"I didn't know you were such a swell dancer," Lily complimented Max.

"There are a lot of things you don't know about me," Max said softly. "But you could find out." Lily batted her dark eyelashes.

Rebecca stifled a giggle as she unwrapped the left-over party cookies. She offered them to Max and Lily and then chose a macaroon for herself.

"These treats are from Rebecca's birthday party on Saturday," Max explained. "She is now an actress at the tender age of ten years and one day!"

"Happy birthday, doll-baby!" Lily said. "You're having quite a celebration."

"It's my best birthday ever," Rebecca agreed. She pushed the cookies to the center of the table. "Here,

Max, you and Lily finish these. I'm going to see if Roddy will let me crank the phonograph."

Roddy let Rebecca choose the next record and wind up the turntable. As the music played, Rebecca stole glances at Max and Lily. They didn't seem to be talking much, but Max was making the same "goo-goo eyes" as in the scene on the patio. Only this time, Rebecca didn't think Max was acting.

Don Herringbone had noticed the couple, too. After one scowling glance, he left the room in a huff.

The afternoon was filled with more filming. "I want to get all the scenes with the kidlet in them," L.B. said. "We've only got one day."

Rebecca sighed. She wondered if she'd ever have a chance to be in a motion picture again.

The crew moved to a different set. Rebecca stepped onto a low platform with a simple backdrop of painted trees. Would it really look like a wooded path in the film?

She concentrated on her scene. "Di-an-a!" she called, moving her mouth in exaggerated motion. When the couple turned, she imitated Rex spying on them, pretending to stroke a mustache. Diana and Gus raised their eyebrows in alarm. Rebecca pointed back toward the mansion, where Rex had gone. Diana sagged against Gus in shock, and he fanned her face with his handkerchief. When Diana recovered, he knelt on one knee, clasped his hands together, and implored Diana to marry him. She batted her eyelashes and nodded as Rebecca gazed at them with a joyful smile.

"Freeze!" shouted L.B., and the trio stood stock still. "And fade! It's a take."

Lily hugged Rebecca. "You were perfect!" she told her. "Your face is so expressive. I worked on that for years, and it comes so naturally to you."

"Now," Max said, "go turn yourself back into Rebecca in the dressing room, and take a nice break. Later we'll go watch the rushes."

"Rushes?" Rebecca asked.

"That's movie talk for film that's been rushed into development," Max explained. "The cameraman develops it in his chemical soup, and later this afternoon we all get to see how it looks. It's hardly ever what you expect!"

Back in Lily's dressing room, Rebecca carefully hung the silky pink gown on a hanger. Borrowing one of Lily's satin robes, she rubbed cold cream on her face and washed it clean. Soon she was back to herself again, in her own dress, cotton stockings, and sturdy shoes. Trying to hang on to the magic of the day, she left her hair in ringlets and kept on her hat. One of the extras brought in two cups and a pot of tea, and Rebecca and Lily spent the rest of the afternoon sipping, talking, and thumbing through moving picture magazines. Rebecca felt deliciously grown-up. She could hardly believe she was the same Rebecca who was nine years old only two days before.

At last a rhythmic knock sounded at the dressing room door. *Rap-rap-a-tap-tap—*

"That's Max," Rebecca said, jumping up. "He always does that." She gave the two responding taps, and Max opened the door.

With one actress on each arm, Max walked Rebecca and Lily down a flight of stairs to a dim, windowless basement room. One wall had white canvas stretched across it. Actors and crew members sat in rows of chairs facing the canvas, and a movie projector buzzed at the back of the room.

"Almost ready," said the cameraman, looping the film along a series of sprockets in the projector.

Don Herringbone came in, accompanied by a pretty young woman who Rebecca guessed was another actress. They took seats apart from the others, talking softly with their heads close together. Max had been right—Mr. Herringbone loved the ladies. All of them!

L.B. entered the room with a fat cigar stuck in his mouth, and silence fell over the group. The director closed the door, plunging the room into complete darkness. Rebecca felt the same thrill she had felt when she watched the Charlie Chaplin film. "Roll it!" L.B. called through his teeth.

The projector whirred and a flickering light came on. A close shot of Lily opened to fill the canvas screen. She stood at the balcony, surrounded by lush flowers.

"There wasn't any flower garden when that scene was shot!" Rebecca whispered to Max.

"Glass plates," Max whispered back. "The flowers are painted on a piece of glass, and the glass is placed in front of the camera lens. It's motion picture magic. The scene in the woods will have a glass plate, too, with leafy trees all around," he explained.

So that's what glass plates were. Rebecca would never have imagined that the flower garden would look so real.

Max entered the scene, holding the white rose and wooing his sweetheart. In a moment, Rebecca saw a young girl in a flowing gown walking toward a vine-covered archway. *That's me!* she thought, her breath catching in her throat. But the girl on the screen looked nothing like her. Rebecca watched the film version of herself go through the scene, her dark eyes revealing each emotion to the audience. There were a few close-up shots where she looked larger than life. In other scenes, the audience saw just a side view with her face partly hidden by her hat.

"Looks good," L.B. announced as the film footage flickered to an end. "Put it in the can."

Lily shook Rebecca's hand. "Congratulations, doll-baby. Now you're a real player."

Rebecca took one last look through the gate as they waited for the bus back to the ferry. "Even if I never get to be in another motion picture, at least my name will be on the screen for this one." Max and Lily looked at her without a word. "Won't it?" Rebecca asked.

Max put his hand on Rebecca's shoulder. "I'm afraid not," he said. "Banbury Cross Studios just started listing the names of the main actors and actresses on the screen. Before that, none of the players' names were listed in the movie. In fact, this is the first time *my* name will appear on the screen."

"Right up there with mine," Lily said, squeezing Max's arm playfully.

"Gosh, my friends will never know that's me in the movie," Rebecca said. Then she reconsidered. "On the other hand, it's probably good that Bubbie will never know. She'd hate having another actor in the family!" Rebecca clapped her hand over her mouth. She hadn't meant to insult Max.

"You mean my own relatives don't respect my theatrical pursuits?" he said, gasping in mock surprise. Then he patted Rebecca's arm. "Don't worry, I already know exactly what they think. They've told me enough times!"

"Oh, Max, I'm sorry," Rebecca stammered.

"Everyone in the family loves you."

"I know." Max shrugged. "They just don't love my job."

Lily nodded in sympathy. "My parents think actors are simply wicked! When they were growing up, it wasn't respectable for women to be in show business. They tried everything to get me to become a bookkeeper. Still, Mama admits that they go to every picture I'm in."

"You see?" Max said. "I just know motion pictures are going to sweep America. There's never been anything like them! And mark my words—if you're a successful actor, people will admire and respect you."

Rebecca imitated Bubbie's frown and accent. "A respectable young lady in a moving pit-cher? *Oy vey!*" Then she grew serious. "I think being an actress would be better than any job in the world—even better than working in the shoe store or being a teacher, as Papa wants me to be." Rebecca sat down on the bus with Max beside her, and Lily took a seat behind them. "Do you think my family would ever let me be an actress?" Rebecca asked.

Max hesitated before answering. "It wouldn't be

easy for them to accept, Rebecca—especially your grandparents."

Rebecca mulled over Max's words. She was heading back to her ordinary life—but she had discovered something inside herself, and she would never be the same. Now she had a dream of acting in motion pictures. Hadn't Max called her "a natural"? Even L.B., the Grand Pooh-Bah himself, had said she was talented.

Rebecca wanted her family to be proud of her always, but if she became an actress, they wouldn't be—at least not at first, and maybe not ever. Rebecca thought back over the past two days. She had given up her wish for a birthday cake when she thought it might be wrong. But it would be much harder to give up her dream of becoming an actress. And as it turned out, having a birthday cake during Passover wasn't wrong after all. Maybe being an actress wasn't wrong, either.

Rebecca glanced over at Max and Lily. They had faced their families' disapproval to do what they loved. Would she?

The actors and crew had nearly all settled onto the bus when Roddy climbed aboard carrying a big box. He stopped by Rebecca's seat. "I heard you reciting the rhyme about Banbury Cross this morning," he said. "You know the rest of it—'With rings on her fingers and bells on her toes, she shall have music wherever she goes.'" He slipped a paper band from one of L.B.'s cigars onto her finger. "I didn't have bells for your toes," he chuckled, "but a lass such as yourself should have music wherever you go." He set the box at her feet.

Rebecca peered inside and saw a shiny red horn. "A phonograph!"

"L.B. wanted you to have a little souvenir from the Prop Room," Roddy said. "Consider it payment for a fine day's work."

"Thank you," Rebecca breathed. Her very own phonograph! She couldn't wait to show Rose.

Darkness enveloped the ferry as Rebecca stepped aboard. Max pointed to the sky. "Where can you always see shooting stars?" he asked. When Rebecca couldn't guess, he slapped his knee. "Why, at a cowboy movie!"

Rebecca laughed. Good old Max—always joking.

The New York skyline grew closer, sparkling with lights. Rebecca was tired, but she was too excited to rest. She looked around at all the actors and crew on the ferry, fixing them in her memory. She hoped she would see them again someday. Above her, she saw millions of stars glittering in the night sky. Maybe one day, she too would be a star, flickering brightly on a silver screen.

A Bar Mitzvah Celebration

CHAPTER 5

s the crisp spring weather gave way to a balmy summer, Rebecca felt a fizzy feeling of wild excitement whenever she thought of her day at the movie studio. Yet somehow, several months had slipped by, and she still hadn't found the right moment to tell her family that she'd played a role in a movie.

Today was definitely not the best time to share the news. It was her brother's turn to steal the limelight. Victor had turned thirteen, the age when Jewish boys were considered full members of the congregation, and today he would join the men in prayer.

"I can't believe you closed the shoe store today, Papa," said Rebecca. "Saturday is your busiest day of the week."

Papa straightened his tie. "It's not every day that

your son becomes a *Bar Mitzvah,"* he said with a note of pride.

Grandpa had been teaching Victor to read the Hebrew prayers since he was eight years old. Grandpa could be a demanding tutor, and he became impatient when Victor made the tiniest mistake. He insisted Victor recite over and over again until each line was perfect. Finally Grandpa had decided that Victor was ready.

Rebecca knew it was an important day for her brother. Still, she was tired of everyone making a fuss over him. Mama let him stay up late to do his homework. Papa brought him to the family's shoe store and let him choose a fancy pair of leather oxfords. And Grandpa spent every extra minute studying with Victor. All the attention had made Victor quite bossy. He yelled at little brother Benny if he made any noise while Victor was studying. He ordered Rebecca and her sisters around when he wanted something to eat or drink. Rebecca tried to stay out of Victor's way, but it was hard in such a small apartment.

Rebecca crept up to her parents' closed bedroom door. Inside, she could hear Victor and Grandpa going over the passage Victor would read aloud from the *Torah,* the ancient scroll that contained the first five books of Jewish Scripture.

Sadie and Sophie quietly joined her at the door. All three strained to hear Victor practicing for the last time. He began chanting the Hebrew words in a mellow tone, when suddenly a high-pitched sound squeaked out of his throat. Her brother's voice had cracked! It sounded as if little Benny had spoken for his older brother. Rebecca nearly burst out laughing. She and the twins stifled their giggles and hurried away from the door.

"I think Victor has a bigger problem than reading the Hebrew words without a mistake," Rebecca said. The girls dissolved into gales of laughter, just as Victor came into the kitchen.

"What's so funny?" he asked, stretching importantly in his new suit.

"You are," Sadie laughed. "You may be a man today, but your voice doesn't seem to know it!"

Victor narrowed his eyes. "Stop trying to make me nervous," he barked. "You're just plain jealous."

"That's enough," Mama interrupted, patting Victor

soothingly on his back. "This is a day to celebrate, not to fight." She shooed everyone toward the door, and the family filed out, with Papa and Grandpa leading the parade.

People dressed in their best clothes strolled along the sidewalk and called out, "Good *Shabbos*!" Rebecca and her family gaily returned the wish for a pleasant Sabbath as they walked to the synagogue on Eldridge Street.

"Doesn't your brother look grown-up in his suit?" Mama asked, but only Benny nodded enthusiastically. "I can't believe he's out of short pants already," Mama sighed. Rebecca and the twins looked at each other and rolled their eyes. *It's Victor this, and Victor that,* Rebecca thought with exasperation. *Victor, Victor, Victor!*

"I'd rather be playing baseball," Victor muttered, but Rebecca thought he was just bluffing. Who wouldn't love being the center of so much attention?

"You couldn't play very well in *that* outfit," Rebecca scoffed.

"I could play in anything," Victor boasted.

"Oh, really? Then so could I!" said Rebecca sarcastically, taunting her brother.

Victor smirked. "Right, I can just see you running around the bases in a dress! You couldn't play baseball if you wore a Yankees uniform."

Rebecca swatted Victor on the arm, but he just strode off and caught up with Papa and Grandpa.

A friend of Grandpa's fell into step behind them, his long beard hanging down onto his shirt.

"Mazel tov!" he congratulated Victor. "I see from the trousers that today you are a man, eh?"

"First he will pray with the men," Grandpa said. "If he doesn't make a mistake, then you can give him a 'mazel tov.' But not yet!"

Victor squirmed and tugged at his jacket. Rebecca knew he was nervous. It wouldn't be easy to stand before the entire congregation and chant the Hebrew passage alone. Victor had practiced hard the past few months, but sometimes he still made mistakes. And what if his voice cracked?

"So, after the prayers, a nice celebration, eh?" persisted the man.

"Nothing fancy," Papa said. "Tomorrow we'll have a family picnic." Rebecca didn't know where the picnic would be, since Papa wanted it to be a surprise. Mama and Bubbie had refused to reveal the secret. Rebecca hoped it was someplace she'd never been before, like Central Park.

"I don't see why everyone is making such a fuss about a Bar Mitzvah," Sadie complained. "And why should boys be the only ones who read from the Torah? If Grandpa had taught me Hebrew, I could do it, too." The springy curl at her forehead bounced as she walked.

"Me, too," Rebecca chimed in. "I'm much better at memorizing than Victor."

"Boys get to do everything," Sadie grumbled, and Sophie nodded in agreement.

"Enough with the *kvetching,*" Mama scolded. She didn't like complaints.

"To be a good Jewish wife and mother, you girls still have plenty to learn," said Bubbie. "You must keep the house kosher and observe the Sabbath every week. The men will do the Torah reading."

Yet Rebecca couldn't help thinking that boys did get to do a lot more than girls, and not only studying Hebrew. Papa let Victor go off to places that even his older sisters weren't allowed to visit alone. And in school, the teachers almost always chose boys to be class monitors or to run errands.

Still, Rebecca had to admit that her brother had worked hard for this special moment. On top of his regular schoolwork each day, Victor had done all the lessons that Grandpa gave him.

As Rebecca approached the wide steps of the synagogue, she saw her cousin Ana waiting with her family. Rebecca started to shout hello, but in the nick of time, she held her tongue and just waved. She knew Mama would scold if she raised her voice in front of the synagogue, even for a greeting.

Cousins Josef and Michael slapped Victor on the shoulder. "Don't worry," Josef said. "We both read from Torah when we turned thirteen back in Russia. Is not so hard!"

"Victor is looking like grown-up," Ana remarked to Rebecca.

"Whatever you do, don't tell him," Rebecca replied. "His head is already too big."

Ana looked critically at Victor. "Head is not too big," she said. "Maybe just ears."

Rebecca smiled fondly. Ana had learned English

well since her family had arrived in America, but she still made some funny mistakes.

As the family opened the heavy wooden doors of the synagogue, cousin Max came around the corner with a young woman on his arm. They didn't have to get any closer for Rebecca to know who it was.

"That's Lillian Armstrong," she whispered to Ana.

"The actress?" Ana gasped. "I can't believe a real actress is coming to your brother's Bar Mitzvah!"

"Shhh!" said Rebecca. "Don't let Bubbie hear. She doesn't think acting is respectable, especially for a lady."

Max introduced Lily to the family. "This is Lillian Aronovich," he said. Rebecca raised her eyebrows in surprise. Lily must have changed her name from Aronovich to Armstrong so that it would sound more American, just as Max had changed his name from Moyshe Shereshevsky to Max Shepard. Bubbie hadn't approved of that, either.

Rebecca was delighted to see that Max and Lily were keeping company. Rebecca wanted to give Lily a hug, but then she would have to explain where she had met Lily before—at the movie studio. The family might decide they didn't approve of Lily, just because she was an actress. Rebecca greeted Lily with a formal handshake, but she broke into a smile when Lily secretly winked at her.

"So, where you two meet each other?" Grandpa asked Max.

"Shouldn't we go in," Rebecca interrupted, "so Victor can get settled?" She didn't want Max to have to explain that he and Lily were working together in a movie. "What a pretty dress, Miss Aronovich," she said quickly.

Lily wore a lacy white summer dress and had covered her hair with a large straw hat. No one would ever guess that beneath the hat, her hair was cropped in a shocking bob. There wasn't a trace of makeup on Lily's face. Rebecca guessed that Lily wanted to make a good impression on the family. It seemed to be working. Mama smiled warmly at Max, and Bubbie allowed Lily to take her arm and escort her inside.

"So, your family comes from Russia?" Bubbie asked.

"They come from Kiev in the Ukraine," said Lily. Bubbie patted Lily's hand approvingly.

In the synagogue, Papa made sure that Victor knew

the proper way to wear the long prayer shawl. He beamed as Victor draped it around his shoulders, but Rebecca noticed that Victor's hands were trembling.

Rebecca headed toward the balcony where the women sat, overlooking the men at prayer. As she started up the stairs, she traced her finger around the bold Star of David carved in the newel post at the foot of the staircase. Behind her, Mama tugged Benny as he tried to pull away. "I want to go with Papa," Benny whined.

"Not until you start learning Hebrew," Mama told him. "And learn to sit still." Benny pouted, and he stomped his feet all the way up the stairs.

As they settled into the front row for the best view, Rebecca gazed at the two enormous stained-glass windows that glowed at each end of the cavernous room. Each round frame held twelve colorful rosettes, one for each of the twelve tribes of Israel. Rebecca felt a sense of peace enveloping her as a hush fell over the congregation.

"Is beautiful here," Ana whispered. "So bright and lovely, and so quiet. Not like our tenement, where everything is dark, and there is noise every minute."

The cantor began to sing a welcoming song, and Rebecca let the sound wash over her. Mama gave Benny a stern look until he stopped swinging his legs. She handed him a prayer book, which he promptly opened, holding the book upside down.

After the opening prayers, the rabbi took the Torah from its special cabinet. The parchment scroll was draped in a velvet covering embroidered in thick gold thread. Setting the cover aside, the rabbi unfurled the parchment scroll until he found the passage for the day.

"Bubbie embroidered the Torah cover," Rebecca whispered in Lily's ear. It was an honor to be asked by the rabbi to work on such a project, and Rebecca was sure Lily would remember to compliment Bubbie on her needlework skills.

With a firm grip, Papa lifted the Torah by the two bottom handles, raising it high in the air while the rabbi intoned in a deep voice, "This is the Torah that Moses placed before the people of Israel." Papa carefully laid the hand-lettered scroll on a high table as the rabbi called Victor by his Hebrew name.

Victor looked pale as he ascended the platform that stood near the front of the synagogue, and Rebecca felt a sympathetic flutter in her own stomach. The platform was like a stage, and today Victor was in the spotlight, but he wasn't acting. This was real.

Victor touched the fringe of his prayer shawl to the Torah and chanted a prayer in a shaky voice. Then he read the Hebrew words, keeping his place with a long silver pointer. His voice grew stronger and his melodic chanting rose up, filling the synagogue. When he had finished, the rabbi led the handshakes. Victor's voice hadn't cracked once, and Rebecca breathed a sigh of relief for her brother.

Papa and Grandpa swelled with pride. Mama dabbed at her eyes with a handkerchief as the women in the balcony leaned forward and offered their good wishes. Rebecca's heart beat faster. Her brother had joined the men now. He was still her annoying brother, but in her eyes, he had grown up considerably.

Benny raced down the stairs as soon as the service ended. He hugged Victor's legs and squealed, "Mazel tov!"

Juice, coffee, and pastries were set out in a side room, and Victor was ushered to the front of the line. He filled a plate and basked in congratulations.

"Such a *mensch*!" said a big woman in a flouncy dress as she pinched Victor's cheek. A red mark glowed where her fingers had squeezed.

Aunt Fannie kissed Victor and began talking excitedly in Yiddish.

"Mama, speak English!" Ana urged her. "If you are speaking always Yiddish, how you will learn English like me?"

Aunt Fannie looked embarrassed. "I think I am speaking English," she explained, "but out from my mouth is coming Yiddish!" Everyone laughed sympathetically.

Max slapped Victor on the back. "You really hit a home run today," he said. "What do you say we go watch the Yankees hit a few next week?"

"Do you really mean it?" Victor asked. "I've been wanting to go to a ball game forever!" He glanced shyly at Lily. "Maybe Miss Aronovich can come, too."

Lily looked rather shocked, and Rebecca wondered if she was acting. "Oh, no," Lily protested. "A ballpark is no place for a lady. Those games are for men!" Bubbie nodded her agreement.

Lily took Max's arm. "It was so nice to meet you

all," she said as they turned to go. "Congratulations, young man." She gave Victor a little peck on the cheek, and he blushed a deep crimson.

"Before you hurry off," Papa said to Max, "are you free tomorrow? We've got a holiday planned, and you're both welcome to join us." Papa leaned toward Max and lowered his voice mysteriously. "You'll be sorry if you miss this little trip."

"Where are we going, Papa?" Benny asked, pulling at his father's sleeve. "Let's go to the park!"

"That's exactly what I have planned," Papa said. "A day at the park." He broke into a grin. "Steeplechase Park."

"At Coney Island?" Victor exclaimed. "Thanks, Pop!"

Rebecca's friends had told her about the splashing waves and wild rides at Coney Island. It sounded like a wonderland, with strange and delightful things to see and do. She had tried to imagine what it was like. Tomorrow, she would find out.

Max caught her eye and leaned closer. "Just the place for you, my little starlet," he said softly. "You're going to be dazzled!"

Steeplechase—The Funny Place

CHAPTER 6

he steamship to Coney Island glided toward the pier, while seagulls soared and wheeled overhead.

"What lucky birds," Rebecca said. "They get to come to Coney Island every day."

The gangplank was lowered, and Ana, Rebecca, and their families joined the crowd of people streaming down the long pier.

"What?" Bubbie grumbled. "Everybody in New York is coming here with us?" She jostled her way along, elbowing anyone who tried to hem her in.

"Look," Rebecca cried. "There's the Funny Face!" She had seen it before on posters advertising Steeplechase Park. In the distance, a huge Funny Face sign loomed over the entrance to the amusement park, its gigantic grin both silly and challenging.

All around, barkers shouted to the crowd. "Step right up, ladies and gentlemen! Come and see the most amazing creatures that have ever called themselves human!" Rebecca saw freakish pictures painted on a large canvas sign. There was a bearded lady, a man with webbed feet, and a "rubber boy" whose bones could bend in half. As she gaped at them, two of the tiniest people Rebecca had ever seen strolled by, pushing a Chihuahua in a baby carriage. When they came to a turnstile, they walked right under it without even bending over. Rebecca couldn't help staring at the odd family.

"Follow me to the beach," Papa said. "First we'll eat, and when the picnic baskets are empty, we'll head inside."

Rebecca and Ana skipped along hand in hand. The fresh salty breeze mixed with the smells of clams, fish, and potatoes frying at sidewalk stands.

"Steeplechase, Steeplechase, the man with the funny face," Rebecca sang. She had heard her friends at school singing the rhyme as they jumped rope, and now she had seen the real Funny Face for herself.

"Hot dogs here!" yelled a man pulling the long

sausages from a steamer. "Get yer Coney Island Red Hots for just a nickel!"

A sea of people swarmed across the beach, and Rebecca's family came to a halt, wondering where they could find space to eat their lunch. Max pointed to the shade of a wooden pier, and the family trooped toward it, their feet sinking into the loose sand with every step.

Two young women dressed in limp wool bathing outfits dashed past them, running toward the splashing surf. Rebecca watched longingly as they hung on to a thick rope that stretched over the waves, laughing and frolicking in the water while holding on for dear life.

Bubbie looked at the bathers romping on the beach. "For shame," she said crossly. "Look at how people behave here—and such clothes! Where are the manners?"

"I want to go in the ocean!" Benny announced. He began pulling off his shoes and stockings.

"You need a bathing suit to go in," Papa told him. "What will you wear today if your clothes get all wet?"

"I'll take them off and *then* go bathing!" Benny declared.

Sadie and Sophie burst out laughing. "Gosh, Benny,"

Sophie chided, "you can't run around without any clothes—even at Coney Island!" She helped Mama and Aunt Fannie arrange the food on a thin blanket they had spread on the sand.

Josef swiped a pickle and took a crunching bite. "Back there is place to rent bathing suits," he said casually. "We could all go in ocean."

Uncle Jacob frowned. "It costs twenty-five cents for one of those crazy outfits. Just for getting wet in!" Josef dropped his head and munched his pickle without another word.

Rebecca did a quick tally. There were eight children and eight adults. If everyone rented a bathing outfit, it would cost four whole dollars! Then she perked up.

"Well, wading is free," she remarked, slipping off her shoes and stockings. "Come on, Benny, let's cool off." Benny grabbed her hand, and Rebecca led him across the sand.

"Don't let go of him!" Mama called. But she didn't have to worry, for all the youngsters were now removing their shoes and stockings and heading toward the water's edge. Benny would have lots of hands holding on to him.

"It's *meshugah*!" Bubbie sputtered. "Everyone has gone crazy!"

The girls held their skirts up to their knees, trying not to get their clothes wet, and the boys rolled up their trousers and jumped over the waves as they splashed ashore. Benny squealed with delight, stamping his feet and slapping his hands against the water.

The sun beat down hotter. "That's enough for me," Rebecca said after a while. "My head is getting too hot, and my feet are getting too cold."

"And I'm starving," Victor said. They trooped back to the blanket.

Lily was sitting primly beside Bubbie, discussing embroidery. Today her hat was held on with a loose scarf that tied under her chin and hid her cropped hair. Rebecca noticed that Lily's scarf had loosened in the sea breeze.

Bubbie mustn't see Lily's hair bob, Rebecca worried. *What will she think?* Rebecca caught Lily's eye and gestured at her own hair until Lily understood her silent message. Lily pulled her scarf tighter until her short hair was safely covered again.

"Eat, eat!" Aunt Fannie urged, and before long, the

lunch had disappeared and the baskets and blankets were packed up. Rebecca brushed sand from between her toes and wiggled back into her stockings. Sadie and Sophie pulled up their stockings and replaced their shoes.

"I can't believe I am dressing in front of strangers," Sophie said, blushing as men with bare shoulders skipped merrily along the sand in the company of women in open-necked bathing outfits.

"At least you are *dressed,*" Bubbie huffed. "Naked feet is bad enough!"

At the entrance to Steeplechase Park, Papa bought combination tickets for the rides. The family entered an enormous glass pavilion. Rebecca gawked at the mirrored carousel in the center, with three tiers of carved, painted animals circling around. A glittering canopy of lights and mirrors covered the entire carousel, and a band organ pumped out lively music. Bells, cymbals, and drums reverberated throughout the pavilion and made Rebecca feel like dancing.

Papa handed the tickets to Victor. Each ticket was good for one turn on the most popular rides. "You're in charge of keeping all the young people together," he said. "And make sure the girls don't ride anything too dangerous."

Victor's voice swelled with confidence. "I'll watch out for everyone," he assured his father, holding the tickets firmly.

Sadie sniffed. "I don't need to be looked after by my little brother," she declared.

Grandpa gestured toward the crush of people. "A young lady shouldn't be on her own in this place."

"And those rides," Bubbie fretted. Clattering rides whizzed overhead. "People acting like monkeys, swinging through the air. You shouldn't step foot on such dangerous contraptions!"

Papa took Bubbie's elbow and steered her away. "We'll leave the wild amusements to the youngsters while we take a walk. I hear there's a beautiful rose garden. We'll all meet back here at four o'clock," he said, handing Victor his pocket watch. Bubbie's face turned red with worry, but she let Papa steer her off.

Benny tugged Mama's arm, pulling toward the bright carousel. "I want to ride a horse!" he cried. "Where's *my* ticket?"

Mama grasped his hand. "You're staying with me," she said flatly. "If you behave all day, then you may ride the carousel," Mama promised.

Benny started to whimper. "Why can't I go with them? I'm big enough."

Poor Benny, thought Rebecca. Life was a lot worse for her little brother than it was for her, even if he was a boy. She couldn't imagine having to stroll through a rose garden when the excitement of Steeplechase Park was beckoning.

"Promise me you'll stay together," Mama said, and the young people murmured their agreement.

"Enjoy your walk through the gardens," Max said to Mama. "I'm taking Lily on the Steeplechase horses. And that's just the beginning!" Lily smiled demurely, but Rebecca saw a sparkle of anticipation in her eyes.

"I want to ride the Steeplechase horses, too," Rebecca said. "Will you come with me, Ana?"

Victor held the tickets close to his chest. "I'll decide what rides you can take," he announced, talking like a schoolteacher. "Some of them might be too dangerous for you."

Rebecca looked impatiently over Victor's shoulder.

Max and Lily were already moving forward in the long line that led to the racecourse. The wooden horses raced down a mechanical track, with two riders on each one. She couldn't spend a day at Coney Island without going on this ride. After all, this was Steeplechase Park!

"It's not dangerous at all," Rebecca argued. "Give us our tickets."

"Let them go," Josef said. "As for me, I am setting my heart on roller coaster. That is much faster than wooden horses." He turned to Michael. "What you say, brother? Shall we wait for a *real* ride?"

Rebecca snatched two tickets from Victor and headed for the line with Ana. "We'll wait for you at the end of the ride!" Victor shouted, but Rebecca barely listened as she and Ana hurried to the Steeplechase.

A small man dressed in the colorful silks of a horse jockey helped the girls onto a wooden horse, and Rebecca felt a shiver of anticipation. She looked down the racecourse. "I wonder how fast we'll go," she said, putting her arms around Ana's waist.

"Like the wind!" Ana grinned. "We will beat you," she called to Max as he and Lily climbed onto their horse. Lily sat at the front, with Max hugging her waist so she wouldn't fall. The jockey blew a bugle blast, and the wooden horses lunged down the track. Ana and Rebecca screamed with delight.

The wind tugged at Rebecca's hat and ruffled her hair as the horse picked up speed. With a lurch in her stomach, she felt the horse plunge down a steep slope. It sped around curves, up and down hills, and over a stream until it came to rest. The ride hadn't taken long, but Rebecca felt as if time had stopped. Riding a real racehorse couldn't be more thrilling than what she had just done.

The girls tripped down a ramp and across a brightly lit stage. A tiny clown cavorted around them, making silly faces. The girls laughed nervously as they exited past a huge statue of a pink and green elephant.

"Over here!" Victor called. Rebecca peered toward the dim area below the stage and saw the others seated in a row. The air crackled with excitement as hundreds of people eagerly watched the lit platform. Rebecca and Ana crowded in and sat down.

Sophie put her finger against her lips. "Wait until you see what's happening up there," she whispered, pointing up at the stage. "You were lucky you didn't get caught."

Before Rebecca had a chance to ask what Sophie meant, Max and Lily strolled across the stage, headed for the exit. The audience began to titter. Just as Lily reached the huge elephant, a gust of air blew up through the floor, blowing her dress high above her knees. Men in the audience whistled.

Lily fell against Max in a swoon, the back of her hand held limply to her forehead. The audience gasped, but Rebecca was sure Lily was just acting. She had practiced scenes like this before. Max supported Lily with one hand and awkwardly pushed down at her skirt with the other.

Just as Lily regained her composure and hurried to leave, the floor dipped. She struggled to regain her balance, clinging to Max for support, when another blast of air whipped up her skirt. The clown ran up on his short legs and gave Max a playful whack with a paddle. Max puffed out his chest and set his fists in a fighting pose. The crowd cheered. Lily held her clasped hands under her chin, batting her eyelashes and admiring her hero. Max chased the clown around the stage. Then he scooped Lily up in his arms and carried her off the stage. The audience went wild, cheering and applauding.

"No one can get the better of Max," Rebecca crowed. "Especially not when there's an audience in front of him!" She pushed out of the row with Ana and the others as an expectant hush settled over the crowd. Another unsuspecting couple was just coming across the stage toward the exit.

Sophie pushed her hands against her skirt. "I'm glad *I* didn't go on the Steeplechase horses," she confessed. "I would die of embarrassment if my skirt blew up like that."

"You can't be embarrassed at Coney Island," Lily laughed. "Oh, you might feel a bit foolish for a minute, but it's all in fun."

"That's why everyone loves to come here," Max added. "You can do things at Coney Island that you would never do at home, because all the rules are turned upside down." Max wiggled his eyebrows. "And now we're off to the Tickle Ride," he grinned. Lily laughed gaily as he whisked her away.

Thrills, Chills, and Skills

CHAPTER 7

I see this wheel from every spot," Ana said, pointing toward the gigantic Ferris wheel that turned slowly above them. "I'm dreaming of seeing the park and the ocean from up in the sky, just like a bird. But I'm afraid it will make me seasick, like the boat to America."

"The Ferris wheel is a sissy ride," Victor said. "Even Benny could go on it."

"That's not very nice," Rebecca said. "I think it looks kind of scary. I'll bet it's the highest ride in the whole park."

"Ana is a girl afraid of everything," said Michael.

"I'm not afraid of going up in the Ferris wheel," Rebecca said. "I'll go with her."

Victor shrugged and led the group to the Ferris wheel. With the attached strings, he tied one ticket onto a button on Ana's dress and another onto Rebecca's sash. "I don't want you losing these," he said. "After all, Papa did put me in charge."

As the girls moved up in line, Ana's sweaty hand gripped Rebecca's. The Ferris wheel towered above them, as tall as a skyscraper. When an empty car stopped in front of them, Ana hung back. "I think I am changing my mind," she said.

"We can't leave now," Rebecca protested, gently nudging her cousin into the swaying car. "Victor and Michael would tease us for the rest of our lives."

Inside the car, large windows covered with wire went around the top half of the cabin, providing a sweeping view in every direction. Rebecca held Ana's hand as more people entered the car. With each footstep, the car swayed. Ana's knuckles turned white as an attendant slid the door shut. Gears cranked and the car lurched up awkwardly, stopping and swinging as the next car was filled. Several times, the car jolted higher, then halted and swayed.

"I am afraid," Ana whimpered. "Let me go off before I fall out!"

"We can't fall out," Rebecca assured her cousin.

"Besides, it's too late to get off. But look, Ana, we're really moving now. No more stopping."

With one graceful movement, the car soared up into the sky and circled lazily over the park. Rebecca felt a feathery, floaty feeling in her stomach. "This must be what it's like to be a seagull," she marveled. "We're flying!"

Ana began to relax and gazed down to the park below. "Ooh!" she squealed. "People down there are like teensy ants. We are biggest people at Coney Island." Rebecca smiled with relief. Ana wasn't going to panic.

When the cars unloaded, Ana looked a bit queasy. She was the first one off when the cabin door opened. "Is wonderful, except for starting and stopping," she told the others when they were back on the ground. "I think I should go one more time, to prove to myself I am not afraid anymore."

Victor shook his head. "We can't always wait around for you two to get off a ride. There's lots more to do, without doing some rides twice." He untied their tickets and shoved them into his pocket as Rebecca seethed with annoyance.

Victor led everyone down an aisle filled with games

of skill. A crash of broken glass startled them, and they turned to see what had happened. Nearby, a long line of people waited at a booth with glasses and dishes stacked up on the counter. A sign overhead said, "If you can't break up your own home, break up ours!" A young man threw a thick goblet, and a pile of dishes toppled to the ground, smashing to smithereens.

"Whatever are they doing?" Sophie gasped. A girl no older than Rebecca shrieked with horrified delight as she shattered an entire row of china plates. The crowd cheered as the barker awarded her a paper fan.

Rebecca blinked in astonishment. At home, everyone was careful not to break a dish, which would be expensive to replace. But at Coney Island, people happily paid to break them!

They moved on, past shooting galleries with rifles aimed at mechanical ducks, and tossing games of all kinds. Wonderful prizes lined the top shelf in each booth, and Rebecca thought it must be swell to go home with one. Suddenly, a row of Kewpie dolls caught her eye.

"Oh," she cried, pointing to the potbellied dolls. "Just look at those impish eyes and that cute tuft of hair. Remember those Kewpies on the cover of my school notebook?" she asked Ana. "I just adore Kewpies."

"Step right up, little lady," cried the barker. "All these little babies want is a good home. For one nickel, you can't lose." He turned to a pyramid of wooden pins set up behind him. "Just knock over these pins with a baseball and you can choose your prize. Everybody's a winner!"

Rebecca hesitated. She didn't have much money, and the game cost five cents. "Where in the world could you get your very own Kewpie for just one buffalo nickel?" asked the barker. Rebecca knew she couldn't buy one for twice as much. Lined up beside the dolls were baseball gloves, boxed cigars, and plush teddy bears. She would definitely choose a Kewpie.

"You could never win this game," Victor scoffed. "You couldn't hit the side of a tenement house with a baseball." A group of boys standing around the booth began to laugh. Rebecca felt her anger rising.

The barker glanced at the boys. "At Coney Island, everyone gets to do something new," he declared. "And you have three tries. Give it a whirl, little lady, and the Kewpie's yours."

"Let's go," Victor said. "We're wasting time."

"You think that only boys can throw?" Rebecca demanded. "What about hopscotch? You need good aim for that. Girls can throw—and aim, too."

"What about hopscotch?" mimicked one of the boys standing nearby.

"Hopscotch?" his friends echoed. They doubled over with laughter, slapping each other on the back.

They'll stop laughing if I win, thought Rebecca. With three chances, she was sure she could do it. She gave Ana her hat to hold, and then pulled a knotted handkerchief from her sash and counted out five pennies. She plunked them on the counter.

The barker set three balls on the counter. "Go to it, sweetheart."

Rebecca picked up the first ball. She eyed the stacked pins carefully, took aim, and threw with all her might. The ball whacked into the backboard without even grazing the pins. *I can do it,* she thought, steadying her nerves. *I have two more tries.*

Rebecca picked up the second ball and felt its weight. Maybe she didn't need to throw as hard as she had thought. She took a step back and threw a gentle toss. The pin at the very top of the pyramid wobbled, but stayed where it was.

"You call that throwing?" one of the boys jeered. He turned to his friends. "She throws just like a girl!"

"She *is* a girl," retorted another, and they all whooped with laughter.

Rebecca's heart was beating out of her chest. It throbbed high into her throat and up to her ears. Her face felt hot. She picked up the last ball, and no one made a sound. This time she used her whole arm, the way she had seen Victor pitch. The ball hit the pins. The top rows tumbled down with a thunderous crash, and the twins gasped. Rebecca thought she had done it—but two pins in the bottom row were left standing.

"Good try," consoled the barker. "And no one leaves without a prize." He handed her a small metal pin with a grinning Funny Face on it. The face that had looked so amusing when she arrived at Steeplechase Park now seemed to be mocking her. "Now that you've got the hang of it," the barker said, "why not try again? This time you're sure to win that Kewpie."

Lily had said that everyone felt foolish at Coney

Island, and it was all in fun. But Rebecca felt completely humiliated, and it didn't seem fun or funny.

"You wasted five whole cents," Victor pointed out. "You should have listened to me."

"Leave me alone!" Rebecca blurted out. Tears welled in her eyes, and she turned away.

"Aww, don't take it so hard," Victor said. "I'm sorry I teased you. It's just that you don't have any practice throwing a baseball."

"Sure," Rebecca said. "Only *boys* can play baseball, right? Girls can't do anything!" A few people turned and stared. They were grinning as wide as the Funny Face, and Rebecca thought they looked horrid.

"I'm leaving," she said. "I'll meet you by the carousel later."

"You can't go off alone," Sadie said. "We promised to stay together."

"And I've got the tickets!" Victor reminded her, but Rebecca didn't care.

Ana caught her arm. "I'll go with you," she offered. "Then we won't really be breaking our promise, because *we'll* be together."

As the girls started to walk away, Rebecca heard the

barker calling out, "Here you go, hot shot, give it a try. You can't lose!" Rebecca glanced back and saw Victor pick up a ball. Then she heard wooden pins crashing and cheers from the boys hanging around the booth. Victor must have won with just one throw.

Striking Out Alone

CHAPTER 8

ow much money do you have?" Rebecca asked Ana. "We should be able to take a few more rides, even without the tickets."

Ana blinked. "I have no money," she said. "Papa doesn't have extra pennies for allowance."

Rebecca felt terrible. She never should have expected Ana to have pocket money. Ana had stayed with her out of loyalty, and she couldn't spoil her cousin's holiday.

"Let's see," Rebecca said, counting the change in her handkerchief. "I've still got ten cents. That's enough for each of us to choose one more ride, or we could get ice cream sodas instead."

Ana looked longingly at the Ferris wheel. "I would love to go up in the sky once more. Ice cream we can get at home, but I might never be at Coney Island again."

Ana was right about the ice cream. But without

the tickets, she could do only one more amusement, and Rebecca wanted to try something different. "How about the fun house? Victor said it's a maze of crazy mirrors and we might never find our way out. But he can't stop us now." She handed her cousin a nickel and kept five pennies.

Ana looked doubtfully at the fun house entrance. "I guess so . . ." Her voice trailed off.

Rebecca thought for a moment. "Maybe I could go through the fun house while you ride the Ferris wheel. Do you think you could go alone?"

Ana lifted her chin. "I'm not afraid of going up anymore."

"I don't see why we can't do separate things," Rebecca said with a shrug. "How could it matter if we each do just one different amusement and then meet up again?"

Ana looked over her shoulder at the Ferris wheel, turning slowly above the noise and din of the park, and she nodded eagerly.

"Good," Rebecca said, pleased with her plan. She pointed to an empty bench outside the fun house. "After your ride, we'll meet back here at that bench."

Ana nodded again and strode toward the Ferris wheel.

Rebecca paid her five cents and giggled her way through the darkened maze. She bumped into black walls that looked like open doorways and followed long passageways that led her in circles. Crazy mirrors showed silly reflections. In one, she had a long head and a neck like a giraffe. In another, she was as short and fat as a pickle barrel. She stumbled across rippling floorboards, trying to make her way through the puzzle of crisscrossing corridors. At last, she stepped out into the sunshine, relieved and delighted.

Rebecca plopped down on the wooden bench to wait for Ana. Just as she leaned back, it suddenly buckled and folded up, and she went sprawling onto the sidewalk. A wave of laughter rose up from a group of bystanders.

What a mean trick! she thought. All those people were just waiting for her to fall off so that they could laugh at her. She stood up and brushed sand from her hands and dress. She was about to stalk away when she thought about what Max would do. He'd never leave an audience without giving a performance.

Rebecca limped back to the bench, imagining that

movie cameras were rolling behind her. She gingerly touched the seat back, and in a few seconds the bench folded and tilted down. Rebecca leapt into the air, jumping back in feigned fright. The crowd howled with laughter, and more people stopped to watch.

Exaggerating every movement, Rebecca walked warily around the bench, stroking it with her hand as if soothing an angry dog. Cautiously, she leaned her elbow against the back. The bench held for a moment, and she grinned with her victory, but then it collapsed, leaving her elbow poised in midair. Rebecca did a little pantomime, pretending she was comfortable leaning on nothing. She lowered her bent arm just a bit, and then again, searching for the bench. The audience, which had grown larger, erupted in a boisterous round of applause.

Rebecca was basking in the attention when the sound of fire horns and clanging bells cut through the air. The crowd drifted away to see what new excitement was unfolding in the park.

Shading her eyes, Rebecca looked around for Ana. Perhaps the line for the Ferris wheel was a long one. But Rebecca had been in the fun house quite a while, and she had performed her bench act after that. Maybe Ana had gotten lost. The horns blared louder and seemed to be drawing closer. Was this just more Coney Island noise, or was something wrong? She knew there had been huge fires at Coney Island in the past. Maybe another dangerous fire was sweeping through the park!

"What's going on?" Rebecca called as knots of people rushed past.

"It's the Ferris wheel," a woman said. "It's broken down."

Rebecca felt a wave of panic. She ran toward the Ferris wheel, pushing through the swelling crowd gawking at the huge ride. The horns and bells fell silent, and Rebecca heard people screaming from the swaying cars. They were screams of fear, not joy.

The riders in the lowest cars had already been rescued, and two burly men cranked a thick handle at the base of the Ferris wheel to bring the next car down. Sweat glistened on their faces. Slowly, another car was lowered and the frightened passengers helped out to safety. Again, the men began cranking. Suddenly Rebecca heard a loud metal clank. The handle had stuck fast. The men stood by helplessly, uncertain how to fix the newest problem.

A fire truck rolled up. Four firemen jumped out and began ratcheting up the ladder. One section after another rose toward the Ferris wheel cars. Higher and higher the ladder reached, stopping just short of the lowest swaying car. The crowd let out a collective gasp as a fireman climbed to the top of the ladder and slid open the cabin door.

Was Ana in that one? She would be in a terrible panic. The cars rocked back and forth—the part of the ride Ana had feared most. *Why did I leave her?* Rebecca thought. *What will I tell Aunt Fannie and Uncle Jacob?*

Rebecca craned her neck and shielded her eyes from the glaring sun, straining to see. Her heart pounded as one passenger and then another was slowly rescued down the ladder. Many were crying as they descended. Those still trapped in other cars shouted for help. Which car was Ana in?

For what seemed like hours, each car was emptied of its riders until only one full car remained. The crowd held its breath as the fireman reached out to the last trapped passenger. In the distance, Rebecca barely made out the figure of a small girl, frozen at the open door.

Reaching New Heights

CHAPTER 9

he crowd grew, and suddenly Rebecca caught sight of Benny, sitting on Papa's shoulders so that he wouldn't be crushed by the throng. She shrank back, trying to hide. But when she saw the worried looks on her family's faces, she waved her hand and called weakly, "Papa, over here!"

"The Ferris wheel's stuck," Benny chirped from his perch.

Mama hugged Rebecca tightly. "Thank goodness you're safe," she cried. "I was afraid you were trapped up there."

"Where are the other children?" Grandpa demanded. "Why you are alone?" But Rebecca didn't have a chance to answer before everyone was firing questions at her.

"Where are Ana and boys?" Aunt Fannie asked. Her voice quivered.

"Were you on the Ferris wheel?" Papa asked.

"Well, I *was* . . ." Rebecca began, ". . . before." Six pairs of worried eyes stared at her. Silence followed, and Rebecca dreaded what had to come next.

Max and Lily found them huddled in a group, and then Victor, Michael, and Josef shoved through the mob, with the twins on their heels.

"What's going on?" Victor asked. He looked at Papa with exasperation. "We *told* her not to leave."

Rebecca looked down at her shoes. "Ana's up there." The words were heavy on her tongue.

Uncle Jacob looked at the fire-truck ladder reaching toward the open door of the last car. Rebecca saw the flicker of recognition in his eyes. He turned to a policeman guarding a wooden barricade separating the crowd from the rescue operation.

"My daughter is in this car," he said, pointing. "I must go to her."

"Sorry, pal," the officer said. "You need training to climb that ladder. It ain't as easy as it looks. Just relax—the fire crew will bring her down."

"She is afraid. Let me go," Uncle Jacob pleaded.

They watched anxiously as a fireman scaled the

ladder and extended his hand toward Ana. She remained frozen in place, just out of reach. After a few minutes, the fireman came down alone. The crowd groaned.

Rebecca stepped up to the policeman, undaunted by his blue uniform and gleaming badge. "My uncle's right," she said. "Ana is petrified of the swaying car. She's never going to let a stranger pull her onto a wobbly ladder. Maybe if she sees a familiar face . . ." She tugged at his sleeve. "Please, sir, I can help her."

The policeman let out a barking laugh. "We've already got one little lady who's afraid of heights. We don't need two, now, do we?"

Papa spoke up. "Her father is a carpenter," he explained. "He's used to ladders and heights."

Mama tried to convince the policeman to let Uncle Jacob climb up, and Bubbie shook a finger at him and argued in Yiddish. Even the onlookers became fired up, shouting out their opinions to be heard above the hubbub and commotion.

Rebecca realized she'd never get permission to climb up to Ana, but somebody had to get up there—and soon. She shivered at the thought of her cousin stuck all alone in the swaying car. Without wasting another minute, Rebecca slipped under the barricade and inched toward the fire truck, hunching down so that she wouldn't be noticed.

"I can't get that kid to budge," reported the fireman, scratching his head under his cap. "She won't say a word, and I can't convince her that she won't fall if I hold on to her."

"What are you gonna do?" a second fireman asked.

"I'll try once more, and if she won't come down on her own, I'll have to make a grab for her and carry her down over my shoulder," the first one said. "She ain't gonna like it much, but I don't see what choice I have."

"That's a risky move when you're so high up," said his partner. "And it's not gonna help if she panics."

I can't let the fireman snatch Ana when she's already petrified with fear, Rebecca thought. She darted behind the uniformed men and crept along next to the fire truck. Firemen stood with their backs to her, craning their necks toward the teetering car.

Rebecca climbed onto the running board and made her way to the back of the truck. She gazed up at the ladder, which wobbled unsteadily. Afraid to think too long about what she was doing, Rebecca began to climb. As her feet reached for each rung, she tried not to look at the wide, empty gap between the steps.

The ladder bobbled, and Rebecca felt a fluttering in her stomach that was much stronger than when she had ridden on the Ferris wheel and held none of the pleasure. The ground receded farther and farther, the crowd below shrinking smaller and smaller. The deafening din of the park seemed muffled and distant.

As Rebecca climbed, she could see her cousin cringing, her face pale. "I'm coming, Ana," Rebecca called. "Don't be afraid." The sea breeze grew stronger as she climbed. One wayward gust caught Rebecca's straw hat and lifted it from her head. She watched helplessly as it sailed through the air toward the mob of people far, far below. Looking down made her head swim, and she quickly fixed her eyes back on Ana. She moved more slowly, gripping the ladder tightly and making certain that each footstep landed squarely on the next rung. She didn't want to follow her hat, sailing down to the onlookers below.

At last, Rebecca approached the tip of the bobbing ladder. It wobbled up and down, while the Ferris wheel car in front of her swayed from side to side. A queasy feeling roiled her stomach.

"Come on, Ana," she coaxed. "Let's get down from here." But Ana didn't even seem to hear her.

"Come, bubeleh," she cooed, repeating one of her grandmother's favorite endearments. Maybe the sound of Yiddish would get through to Ana.

Her cousin blinked. "Rebecca!" she breathed hoarsely. "I can't get down."

Rebecca reached out, and Ana's trembling hand met hers. It was cold and clammy.

"Everyone's waiting for us," Rebecca said with a brightness she didn't feel. "We'll go get a cool drink. Wouldn't you like that?" Ana didn't move, but Rebecca could tell she was listening. "Turn around, and climb down backward. I'll hold on to you and guide you onto the ladder." Ana seemed to be considering the suggestion.

"Climbing this ladder is the best amusement in all of Steeplechase Park!" Rebecca went on. "Just think, the boys are going to be *so* jealous of us."

Ana let go of Rebecca's hand and slowly turned around. Planting her own feet carefully and holding on with one hand, Rebecca extended an arm toward her cousin. As she did so, a sinewy hand reached up and gripped Rebecca's waist. Startled, she glanced behind her and saw a husky fireman standing one rung below. In her concentration on Ana, she hadn't noticed him at all. Relief flooded through her, but she kept up her banter to keep Ana calm.

"The first step is the best," Rebecca said. "After that it gets *too* easy. Even Benny could do it."

Gingerly, Ana set her foot down, and Rebecca guided it onto the rung. Then Ana placed her other foot on the ladder. Rebecca held on to Ana's waist firmly, and with a squeaky yelp, Ana released her hold on the swaying car. Back down the ladder they went, one slow step at a time. Rebecca steadied Ana, and the fireman held on to Rebecca.

A roar went up from the gathering below as Rebecca and Ana were lifted off the truck onto solid ground. The entire family rushed to embrace them. Tears ran down Aunt Fannie's cheeks as she enfolded Ana in her arms.

Bubbie fanned herself furiously with a paper fan emblazoned with a grinning Funny Face. "So dangerous," she kept repeating. She looked around and complained to anyone who would listen, "This Coney Island, it's meshugah!"

Benny hugged Rebecca's knees. It was just the way he had hugged Victor after the Bar Mitzvah service, Rebecca thought. That seemed like weeks ago instead of just yesterday.

"Take *me* up the ladder, too!" Benny crowed. "I wanna climb up to the tippety top!"

A policeman stepped up and handed Rebecca her flyaway hat. "Saints preserve us, I wouldn't have believed it if I hadn't seen it with me own two eyes," he said. "One little lass rescuing another."

Rebecca turned gratefully to the fireman who had helped them down. She shook his hand and felt her own disappear into his massive palm.

"We've got to catch our breath," Papa said. "Let's go to Feltman's Restaurant for a cold glass of lemonade."

"I think I need something a little stronger than lemonade," Max chuckled. "You girls gave us quite a scare."

Lily held on to Max's arm as they walked, not realizing her scarf had fallen in limp folds across her shoulders. Everyone who looked in her direction seemed startled by her short hairdo. Bubbie's eyes widened for a moment, and Rebecca held her breath. But Bubbie simply looked heavenward without uttering one word of reproach.

"Look!" Benny cried, pointing at a carousel of carved horses gleaming with colorful jeweled trappings. "Those horses have real tails!" The family walked past Feltman's dazzling carousel and settled at a large outdoor table. Benny tugged at Mama's dress. "I didn't get to ride on the carousel," he wailed. "And I was good all day."

"I think we've had enough rides," Mama said, talking over the vibrant organ music of the carousel.

Benny slumped forlornly in his chair. "No fair!" he complained.

"Did you hear about the daring rescue?" asked the waitress after Papa ordered their drinks.

"First-hand, I'm afraid," Papa replied. He pointed to Rebecca and Ana. "I watched the whole thing. You see, it was my daughter who rescued my niece."

"Heavens to Betsy!" exclaimed the waitress. She turned to Rebecca and Ana. "You two are the talk of Coney Island—and here you are right at my table!"

The waitress returned in a few moments with a tray of glasses and a large pitcher of icy lemonade. "Mr. Feltman says this is on the house," she announced grandly. "It's not every day we have a hero in our restaurant—or should I say, a *heroine*." Then she dropped a string of tickets onto the tray. "And these are for the carousel. Mr. Feltman wants you all to have a ride."

Benny jumped up, nearly toppling his chair. "I'm going to pick the biggest horse!"

When the waitress left, Papa fixed his gaze on Rebecca and Victor. "Mama and I told you children to stay together."

Rebecca hung her head. "I'm sorry, Papa. I really am."

Ana reached for Rebecca's hand, and Rebecca could feel that her cousin was still trembling. "It wasn't only Rebecca's fault," Ana said softly. "I wanted to ride on Ferris wheel one more time. We both broke our promise." She looked up, her bottom lip quivering slightly.

"You both made a serious mistake by going off alone," he said. Giving Rebecca a stern look, Papa slapped the table for emphasis. "Leaving the others was bad enough, but climbing up the ladder was terribly dangerous."

"But Papa," she protested, "I was sure that I could rescue Ana. How could that be wrong?"

Papa's expression softened, and Rebecca thought perhaps she saw a glimmer of pride in his eyes. He hesitated before he finally spoke. "You shouldn't disobey a police officer or put yourself in danger. Still, you did get Ana down, and thank goodness you're both safe now."

Lily nodded, her expression serious. "Sometimes we have to do what we think is right," she said quietly, "even if we don't do what's expected of us."

Rebecca felt confused. "How will I know when it's one of those times?"

Her question hung in the air for a moment. "I guess figuring that out is part of growing up," Papa said finally. He looked at the young people, and then let his gaze rest on Rebecca. "And you are growing up faster than I ever imagined."

"I'm growing up, too," Benny said. "So can I ride the carousel all by myself?"

"Maybe if you take Ana and Rebecca with you—and keep a close eye on them," Mama said with a smile.

Ana gave Rebecca's hand a light squeeze. "We are

just like sisters," she whispered to Rebecca, "together in everything." Rebecca squeezed back.

Max raised his glass. "Here's to Rebecca," he toasted, "who rose above the crowd today."

"She and Ana reached new heights," Lily chimed in, clinking her glass against Max's. "People say anything can happen at Coney Island, and I guess it does!"

"I'll have to agree with that," Mama said. "I never thought I'd see Grandpa playing a carnival game."

Rebecca turned to Grandpa in surprise. "You played a game?"

"Dishes game," Grandpa replied with a sparkle in his eye. "Pay your nickel and break the dishes!"

"*Oy!* Such a clatter!" Bubbie exclaimed. "Real china, crashing and breaking all over. Such a mess like you've never seen!"

Grandpa gave Bubbie a tender pinch on her cheek. "You liked it, too," he chuckled.

"Bubbie!" squealed Sadie and Sophie in amazement. "You broke *dishes*?"

Bubbie shrugged and sipped her drink with a mysterious smile. "How you think I won this fan?" She nudged Grandpa with the folded fan. "This

Mr. Feltman, he wants us to ride his carousel. It's meshugah, but maybe just a *little* ride, to make Mr. Feltman happy."

Rebecca, Ana, and the twins began to giggle. Were Bubbie and Grandpa really going to ride the carousel? Everything *did* seem topsy-turvy at Coney Island!

Victor held up a baseball glove. "Look, Pop, I won this at a throwing game with just one try. Isn't it a beaut?"

Rebecca's smile faded and she stiffened, remembering how she had lost after three tries. "I'd like to know why only boys play baseball, and not girls," she demanded.

"Actually, with a little practice, you could be a decent pitcher," Victor said generously.

"Hmph," Rebecca said. "Well, if I ever do win that throwing game, I sure won't pick a stupid baseball glove." She slurped her drink noisily.

Victor shrugged. "The game was so easy, I played twice," he said. "And I won the second time, too."

Rebecca groaned. "I suppose you took the box of cigars then," she said sarcastically. "After all, now you're a *man*, aren't you?"

Victor gave her a sheepish smile. "Look, I'm sorry

I teased you back there," he said. "That was just a game. But when you climbed that ladder—that was really something."

At this rare praise from her brother, Rebecca felt all her anger drain out of her. "You deserved the glove," she admitted. Then she blurted out something she had been holding back. "You did a good job with your reading yesterday." She swallowed hard. "I was proud of you."

"What's this?" Papa said. "Victor and Rebecca are paying each other compliments? So it's true—anything *can* happen at Coney Island!"

Josef elbowed Victor. "Go on," he murmured.

"Show her," Michael urged.

With a mischievous grin, Victor slowly pulled a Kewpie doll from his pocket and handed it to Rebecca.

"You won this for me?" she asked. Rebecca hugged the doll close. Then she did something she hadn't done in a long time—she hugged her brother, too.

Movie Acting

CHAPTER 10

fter their Ferris-wheel adventure, Rebecca and Ana were as inseparable as Sadie and Sophie. They spent nearly every day together, playing games and sharing secrets. One day, Rebecca told Ana her biggest secret of all—that she had acted in a real moving picture!

At first, Ana rolled her eyes. "You are—how you say—kidding, right?"

"No! I mean, yes! I mean, yes, that *is* how you say it—but no, I'm not kidding!" Rebecca sputtered, giddy with excitement. "And I'll prove it to you. Ask your parents if you can come to the movies tomorrow with me, Cousin Max, and Lily. Then you'll see! But you have to promise to keep my role a secret."

Ana nodded solemnly, but her eyes sparkled. "I promise!"

The piano player near the stage plinked out a sweet melody as the final scenes of *The Suitor* flickered to a close. Rebecca cracked open a peanut shell with her teeth and munched the peanuts, her eyes glued to the glowing movie screen at the front of the theater. A large circle framed the two film sweethearts, then grew smaller and winked shut just as the couple was about to kiss. Boys in the audience whistled at the romantic ending, and girls sighed.

As the piano player ended with a rousing flourish, Ana leaned close to Rebecca. "It's so exciting. To think that I am watching you on the movie screen—with Max and Lily, too! I can hardly believe it."

Rebecca grinned. "I can barely believe it myself." She glanced at Max and Lily, sitting beside her in the theater, and thought back with pleasure to the day she had spent with them at Banbury Cross Studios. Although she had only spent one day on the set, watching the movie now made it seem like everlasting magic.

The lights in the theater came on, and ushers

strode down the aisle, making sure the audience left. "Everyone move to the exits!" the ushers called. They reached beneath the seats and pulled out a few boys who had tried to hide until the next show started.

As Rebecca moved into the aisle, she noticed some people staring curiously at Max and Lily as if the pair looked familiar. But without Lily's long, curly wig and Max's cap and gardener's clothes, no one quite recognized that they were the stars of the moving picture that had just ended.

"Thank you for taking us to see the movie," Rebecca said. "I couldn't imagine what it would look like, since I only acted in a few scenes."

"It's always a bit of a surprise to see how everything fits together when it's done," Max said.

Lily turned to Ana. "How exciting that Rebecca let you in on her secret," she said.

"I don't know how she can keep this to herself," Ana marveled. "I would want to tell *everyone* if I were in a moving picture."

"I wish my whole family could see it," Rebecca admitted. "But you know how my parents and grandparents feel about movies. They think acting isn't respectable, especially for ladies." Her voice faltered. "Someday I'll tell them . . . but I'm not sure when."

Lily smiled at Max mysteriously. "That's what secrets are all about," she said. "Exciting news that you can only share at the right moment."

Rebecca savored the memory of her acting role. "It doesn't matter if no one else ever knows," she said. "I loved being in that movie."

Their feet crunched over discarded peanut shells and candy wrappers as they made their way up the crowded aisle. Outside, the humid August air was thick with heat. Lily waved a paper fan close to her face.

"I had forgotten how hot it is," Rebecca said. "The rest of the world just seems to disappear while I'm watching a movie."

"That's why moving pictures are so popular," Max pointed out. "They let people forget their troubles for a little while."

Lily took Max's arm as they turned to go. "We'll see you two at the Labor Day picnic next week," she said. "The whole studio crew is going, Rebecca, so you'll get to visit with everyone again."

"And don't worry," Max added. "We'll warn them

that mum's the word about your movie role. Your secret is safe with us."

Rebecca hugged Max and Lily good-bye, and the girls headed down the bustling sidewalk to Ana's tenement.

"Max is right about forgetting all your troubles at a movie," said Ana. "If only my parents would go and enjoy themselves, instead of worrying all the time."

"What are they worried about?" Rebecca asked.

"Jobs and money," Ana answered. "Papa and Josef are not paid fairly at the coat factory. No one is. The workers are asking for better pay. If the bosses don't agree, the workers might go on strike. Then Papa and Josef won't earn any money at all."

"Then let's hope there won't be a strike," said Rebecca. She knew Ana's family earned barely enough to make ends meet. Without Uncle Jacob and Josef working, the family would be in serious trouble.

Ana looked so worried that Rebecca wanted to cheer her up. "I've got a great idea," she said. "Let's act out a movie about a worker in a coat factory. Movies have happy endings, so in ours everyone will get a raise."

Ana perked up. "That sounds good! And since I know what the factories are like, I could play the boss."

The girls bounded up the front stoop and into Ana's tenement building. The smells of cooked cabbage and stale garbage filled the dark hallway, and the girls covered their noses and mouths with their hands, trying not to breathe. Straining to see, Rebecca followed her cousin up two flights of creaky wooden stairs. In the tiny, run-down apartment, Aunt Fannie had cleaned everything to a shine, and Uncle Jacob had painted the kitchen walls a sunny yellow.

"Where is everyone?" asked Rebecca, looking around the apartment.

"I don't know," Ana replied. "It's Sunday, so Papa and Josef have the day off. I guess they all decided to go out for a while. If we practice now, maybe we can perform our movie for them when they get home." Ana took one of her father's hats from a nail on the wall and plopped it on her head. "I'll be Mr. Simon. He's the boss." She draped her mother's shawl around Rebecca's shoulders and sat her at a small table in the tiny parlor. "You can be a poor stitcher who's just come to America."

"Okay," Rebecca said. "I'm Katerina Kofsky, fresh

off the boat at Ellis Island." Rebecca bent over the table as if she were leaning over a sewing machine. "*Whirrrrrr,*" she murmured softly, pretending to guide fabric under a needle.

"You really have to slump over," Ana directed. "Look as if you're too tired and hot to even push the fabric through."

Rebecca followed Ana's instructions, imagining that her shoulders ached from bending over the machine. She didn't need to imagine working in stifling heat, since Ana's apartment was so hot and stuffy, it didn't seem as if a factory sweatshop could be any worse.

Ana strode back and forth, her eyes fixed on Rebecca. "Faster! Faster!" she ordered. "You're too slow."

Rebecca really was sweating. She reached up and wiped the perspiration from her forehead.

"Aha!" Ana shouted, pointing an accusing finger. "You are not allowed to stop your machine without my permission, Miss Kofsky!" Ana pretended to pull out a notebook and write in it. "You will lose one hour of pay this week."

Rebecca clasped her hands together. "Please, Mr. Simon," she begged, "I was only wiping off my forehead so I could see the work better. Don't take any money from my pay. If my family can't pay the rent, the landlord will throw us onto the street!"

"And no talking!" Ana gave a mean smile. "I will be kind to you, Miss Kofsky, and only take out a nickel for talking instead of working."

"Not *more* from my pay," Rebecca cried. She leaned over and pretended to sew again. "Oh, please, Mr. Simon. I am working hard."

"Still talking?" Ana made scribbling motions in her imaginary notebook. "That's another nickel! Soon you will learn to do what Simon says." She let out a nasty chuckle.

"What?" Rebecca was indignant. "How can you punish me for nothing? If you don't treat the workers fairly, we will walk out of this factory and go on strike. Then you'll be sorry."

Ana sneered. "Go ahead and strike. There are plenty more workers coming off the boat who will take this job in a minute. I don't need you or your complaints." She pointed to the door. "You do what I tell you, or you're fired."

Rebecca's heart was beating fast. No matter what

she said, Ana seemed to get the better of her. Rebecca couldn't think of what to say next. "Why are you being so mean, Ana?" she sputtered. "In our movie, the workers are supposed to get a raise. You're not playing fair!"

Ana folded her arms across her chest. "I'm not Ana—I'm Mr. Simon. That means I can do whatever I want, and you have to go along with it."

Anger rose in Rebecca's chest. She couldn't do anything without being punished. The movie wasn't fun anymore.

"CUT!" Rebecca yelled, so loudly that her cousin flinched. Rebecca pulled off the shawl. "Why are you doing this, Ana?"

"I'm acting in a movie, just like you said," Ana replied. "I'm being a factory boss."

"Well, you don't have to be so mean," Rebecca protested. "And so unfair."

Ana shrugged. "Josef tells me lots of stories about the factory, and that's how the bosses are."

Surely Ana was exaggerating, but Rebecca didn't want to argue. "Maybe we should play something else," she suggested.

Just then the door opened. Ana's mother and her

brother Michael entered the apartment.

"How was picture show?" Aunt Fannie asked. "Someday I am going to see a movie for myself."

"Oh, Mama, it was wonderful," said Ana, her face glowing. "The movie seemed almost real, and the actors were so good. You should have seen Max and Lily and—" Rebecca nudged her cousin, reminding her of their secret. Ana's unfinished sentence hung in the air.

"While you were at the movies, we went to an important workers' meeting," Michael told his sister. "People gave speeches about how to make the clothing shops better places to work. If the bosses don't change things, there's going to be a huge strike." His eyes shone with excitement.

Aunt Fannie filled a glass with water and sat at the kitchen table. Her face was flushed with heat. "The hall is so packed, we must stand the whole time," she said, "but we stay and hear every word." She took a long drink and said to Ana, "Your papa and Josef, they are still at meeting. Workers from their factory are discussing what to do."

"An Italian girl talked about the Uptown Coat Company, where Papa and Josef work," Michael told them.

"She said it was so hot this week, one of the stitchers fainted right onto the floor, but the other workers were not allowed to stop sewing and bring her some water." His voice rose. "When one girl left her machine to help, the boss fired them both!"

"Why would he do that?" Rebecca asked.

"He said they were wasting time instead of working," Michael said.

"These factories are not fit for human beings," Aunt Fannie said. "Things have to change, but all we hear is talk." She shook her head. "One young stitcher said the time for talking is over—now it is time to *do* something."

"That was Clara Adler," Michael said. "She's not much older than your sisters, Rebecca, but boy, does she have *chutzpah*. When she said the workers must walk out and *force* the bosses to make changes, everyone cheered." His voice was full of fire. "Clara shouted out, 'Either they change, or we strike!' "

Rebecca almost felt like cheering, too, just listening to Michael. If all the workers walked out together, that would show those bosses they couldn't get away with being so unfair! Then she remembered what Ana had said—the bosses could just hire new workers, and nothing would change. "Do you really think a strike would help?"

"It's the only thing left to do," Michael insisted. "Things can't get any worse than they are now."

"Yes, they can," Aunt Fannie said quietly. "If your papa and Josef can't bring home the pay every week, things will be a lot worse—for us."

Inside the Factory

CHAPTER 11

n Monday afternoon, Ana and Rebecca sat on the stoop in front of Ana's tenement, hoping it might be cooler outside.

"They're going to have games and races at the Labor Day celebration," Rebecca said. "If we practice the three-legged race, maybe we'll win." She took the ribbon from her hair and tied her right leg to Ana's left leg. With their arms around each other's waists, they tried to step in unison. At first they stumbled a bit, but soon they began to pick up their stride. Down the block they went, stumping along and feeling so silly, they couldn't stop giggling. But the heat was stronger than they were, and soon they headed back upstairs for a drink.

"Come take a look at this shelf," Michael called from the fire escape outside the open parlor window.

Rebecca peered out, wrinkling her nose at the pungent smell of paint and turpentine. Old newspapers covered the iron grate, and a freshly painted wooden shelf lay on top. Michael finished one last brushstroke and then swished his brush in a can of turpentine. He glanced up at the sky. "I don't know how this shelf will dry when the air feels wetter than the paint." He leaned back and looked at his work. "I think dark blue is the nicest color so far."

Rebecca admired the piece, which had three perfectly joined shelves and a swirly design carved at the top. "Are you going to hang it in the apartment?" she asked.

Aunt Fannie came over, wiping her hands on her apron. "Your Uncle Jacob is fine carpenter," she said. "He made that shelf for us." She pointed toward the kitchen, and Rebecca saw a sunny yellow shelf hanging on the wall over the work sink. It was just like the one Michael was painting. "Neighbors see this shelf and admire," Aunt Fannie went on. "Then your uncle has genius idea to build shelves to sell to other renters."

"When we have a bigger place to live, my father will have a real workroom, with plenty of space for his tools," Michael said. "Then he'll be able to make cabinets and tables, too."

Rebecca wondered how Uncle Jacob would be able to afford a larger apartment. If he got a raise, perhaps the family could move.

Michael started to clean up the newspapers when something grabbed his attention. "Look! Here's a picture of Clara Adler in the newspaper," he called, handing the wrinkled paper through the window.

"Let's see," Rebecca said, smoothing out the wrinkles and holding the paper up for Ana and Aunt Fannie. Clara did look quite young, but Rebecca detected a look of steely determination in Clara's eyes as she stood on a stage speaking to other workers. Rebecca glanced at the headlines. "Honest Pay for Honest Work," read one. "Factories Are Fire Hazards," warned another.

Rebecca began reading. "Why, these are letters that ordinary people wrote to the newspaper," she marveled. Each one contained a different opinion about the clothing factories. "Listen to this: 'Dear Editor, At my job we are not allowed to use the bathroom, except during our short lunchtime. Then so many girls are lined up, there is no time to eat, except while we stand and wait our turn for the bathroom.' " Rebecca looked up. "That's terrible. How could any place be so mean?"

"Clara Adler wants to change that by organizing the coat workers to strike," Michael said with admiration. "Now there's a girl who does a lot more than just complain!"

Aunt Fannie returned to the kitchen and finished packing food into two covered baskets. "I know that *our* workers will complain if we don't bring them something to eat tonight." She held the baskets out to Ana. "Take your father and brother their suppers before it gets any later."

"Why didn't they bring their suppers with them when they went to work?" asked Rebecca.

"Factory is too hot for food to sit out all day long," Aunt Fannie replied. "Without icebox, their suppers would spoil by evening."

Rebecca was curious to see if the factory was really as bad as Ana and Aunt Fannie described it. "May I go too?" she asked. Aunt Fannie hesitated, but Rebecca persisted. "I'll go home as soon as we deliver the baskets," she promised, and Aunt Fannie agreed.

Outside, heat radiated from the sidewalk, and

Rebecca felt as if she were pushing against a wall of wet cotton. Damp ringlets of hair stuck to the back of her neck.

"I'm glad you're coming with me," Ana said. "I always feel a tiny bit scared when I go. As soon as I open the front door, the noisy machines sound like growling animals."

"It can't be that bad," Rebecca declared. "My parents worked in a shoe factory when they first came to America, and Mama jokes about it. She says that she and Papa fell in love over a pile of shoes, and that's why they are a perfect pair."

Farther up the block, Rebecca noticed a river of water running down the gutter next to the sidewalk. When the girls turned the corner, they saw a gushing fire hydrant. Kids of all ages were splashing in the water, shouting and squealing with delight. In the middle of the street, a horse pulling a delivery wagon had stopped to drink from a shallow puddle.

"An open fire hydrant!" Rebecca exclaimed. "Let's run through and cool off!" Ana didn't need to be convinced. With a whoop, the cousins darted into the spray and gasped as the cold water hit them.

"My stockings are soggy, but it feels wonderful!" Rebecca said gleefully as they left the boisterous hubbub behind.

"I'll bet this is the hottest day of the whole summer," said Ana. "I think I'll sleep on the fire escape tonight. It's much cooler than sleeping in the tenement. Lots of kids sleep outside, so it's almost like a party." Her eyebrows lifted. "Maybe you could sleep over tomorrow night!"

Rebecca's eyes lit up. "Oh, I hope Mama will let me!" She imagined what it would be like looking at stars overhead as she went to sleep.

After several blocks, Rebecca saw a tall brick building ahead. It cast a deep shadow across the sidewalk and street. A huge sign on the building read *Uptown Coat Company.*

Ana pulled open the heavy metal door, and the cousins stepped into the gloomy entryway. Carefully, they climbed up six steep flights of rickety stairs. A humming noise, like a swarm of angry bees, grew louder as they approached the top.

"I can see why you don't like coming here," Rebecca admitted. "This place gives me the willies." A thick blanket of heat pressed against her, and Rebecca felt as if she couldn't breathe. But she had come this far, and she wasn't going to turn back now.

Ana pointed to a door. Black letters painted on the smoked glass said *Private—No Admittance.*

"That's Mr. Simon's office," Ana said, speaking loudly into Rebecca's ear so that she could be heard above the sound of buzzing machines. "Josef says he has nice big windows in there and a fancy electric fan right on his desk." Rebecca followed Ana toward a solid metal door at the end of the hallway. "That's where my papa works and where Josef picks up bundles to deliver."

The metal door opened with a grating sound, and a stooped man staggered out, balancing a heavy pile of coats on his back. The door thudded shut behind him, and Rebecca moved out of his way.

Ana rushed forward. "Josef!" she cried.

Rebecca couldn't believe it was Ana's brother. His face was lined and his skin looked pasty gray. He nodded at them as he shuffled by.

"We've brought your dinner," Ana said, but Josef didn't answer. He struggled down the steep staircase trying to carry the load of coats.

Rebecca remembered Ana playing the boss and fining her just for talking. Would Josef have money taken from his pay if he just said hello to his sister?

A balding man with a potbelly stepped up to them as the girls opened the metal door to the workroom. "No kids in here," he barked. "Too dangerous." He snapped his suspenders against his chest.

Rebecca stepped back, covering her nose and mouth. The sour odors of sweat and machine oil blended into one foul smell. She would never have believed that the smell and the heat could be worse than in the tenement. Inside the huge loft, men with curved knives leaned over wide tables. They sliced swiftly through layers of thick fabric, their hands nearly a blur. Endless rows of young women in long-sleeved shirtwaists bent over clattering black machines. Everyone worked silently, unable to talk over the room's deafening roar.

Ana spoke up to the foreman. "We're bringing suppers for Jacob and Josef Rubin."

"I'll take those," the foreman muttered.

Rebecca searched the room for her uncle. As her eyes adjusted to the shadowy light, she saw him leaning over a worktable, expertly slicing a stack of cloth. He winked at the girls as the foreman took the baskets.

Rebecca tried to imagine what it would be like working here from early in the morning until late at night. The windows were covered with a layer of grime, shutting out the sunlight. A few dim electric bulbs hung down from the ceiling. Thick dust clung to every surface, and fine particles of lint floated in the sticky air.

One young woman glanced up furtively just before the boss pushed the door shut. She didn't look any older than Sadie and Sophie, but her face was drawn and her eyes dull. Rebecca felt enveloped in sadness. It didn't seem right for her to be looking in at the workers, knowing she could leave after just a few minutes. It was as if they were trapped inside the factory. How could Uncle Jacob stand working in this room for hours and hours, and return to the same drudgery day after day? How could anyone?

Rebecca breathed deeply when she and Ana were back outside. "If it's too dangerous for us to bring your father his dinner, how can they let people *work* in there?" she fumed. "Oh, Ana, I used to laugh when my mother joked about working in a factory, but it will never seem funny again."

"I wish Papa and Josef didn't have to work there," Ana said. "But even if they found jobs at a different factory, it would be just as bad. Maybe someday they will be able to leave . . ." Her voice trailed off.

There was nothing else to say. As terrible as the factory was, Rebecca understood that Uncle Jacob and Josef needed their jobs. They were trapped, like the other workers.

Rebecca remembered the steely glint in Clara Adler's eyes. Complaining wouldn't change anything. Something had to be done.

City Tree House

CHAPTER 12

On Tuesday, Rebecca ate her lunch as fast as she could and finished all her chores in record time. In spite of the heat, she felt a shiver of excitement as she stuffed her pajamas into her calico bag. Tonight she was going to sleep out on the fire escape with Ana.

"This is going to be the best day of the week," she exclaimed.

"Don't forget these." Mama handed Rebecca her toothbrush and a tin of tooth powder. Rebecca dropped the items into her bag and quickly tucked in a folded piece of paper. The paper held a secret she was going to share with Ana when they were alone.

"It's clouding up," Mama said. "Maybe we'll finally get some rain."

Rebecca groaned. "That would spoil everything!"

She hurried to the door, clutching her bag. "On the other hand, now that I think about it, who cares if it pours? I'm so hot, I'd love to get caught in a thunderstorm. *Oooh*—wouldn't it feel delicious?"

Mama just shook her head and gave Rebecca a kiss good-bye. "You two be careful on the fire escape," she cautioned. "I want you home tomorrow safe and sound!"

By the time Rebecca knocked on Ana's door, the threatening clouds had thinned and a few rays of pale sunshine struggled to break through the humid haze.

If only there were more windows in the tenement, it would be a little cooler inside, Rebecca thought as she entered Ana's stifling apartment. But tonight it wouldn't matter. She and Ana would be outside, breathing the fresh night air.

"How about making some lemonade?" Aunt Fannie asked, placing a sack of overripe lemons on the table. "Maybe a drink will cool us off."

Ana took a glass juicer from a shelf, and Rebecca sliced lemons in half while Ana rotated each piece back and forth across the pointed tip of the juicer. The lemons were squishy-ripe with a few brown spots, and Rebecca guessed that Aunt Fannie had gotten them from a street peddler at a bargain. Tart, frothy juice dripped into the bottom of the glass dish. When it was filled, the girls carefully poured the juice into a pitcher through a fine sieve that caught the seeds. They mixed in water and sugar and took turns stirring until the sugar dissolved.

Ana chipped a chunk of ice from the block in the icebox and dropped it into the pitcher. "I really need a *cold* drink!" she said.

"Don't waste ice," Aunt Fannie scolded. "It's bad enough in this heat that I have to pay iceman every day. Maybe you believe old stories that in America, the streets are paved with gold!"

Aunt Fannie brought out a loaf of dark bread. "It is too hot to cook, so I hope a light supper will be enough." She took a jar of pickled herring from the icebox and began slicing some tomatoes. Rebecca hoped the small meal was really because of the heat and not because Aunt Fannie couldn't afford anything more.

Supper was over quickly. After Rebecca and Ana washed and dried the dishes, they helped Michael cover the opening to the emergency stairs on the fire escape with some boards.

Michael glanced up at the cloudy sky. "If you two sleep out tonight, you may get a good bath, too." He made sure the boards were firmly in place and then grinned mischievously. "If you don't get washed away by a thunderstorm first, this should keep you from falling through." He leaned over the edge of the railing and gave a long whistle that got lower and lower in pitch. "It's a long way down."

Ignoring her brother's teasing, Ana climbed back through the window and dragged a feather bed from a corner of the parlor. She pushed while Rebecca pulled it through the window and onto the fire escape. Aunt Fannie handed out a sheet and two soft pillows. Up and down the block, Rebecca saw other children setting up beds outside. They began to banter and call over the railings.

"Catch!" a tall girl in the next building shouted to Ana. She tossed a red rubber ball across the space between them. Ana caught the ball in both hands and then tossed it back. The game lasted until the ball was missed and went tumbling down, bumping against jutting fire escapes until it hit the pavement below.

"Finders keepers!" shouted a skinny boy playing on

the street. Then he laughed. "Just kidding." He heaved the ball as high as he could, and it bounced onto the girl's fire escape.

When it began to grow dark, Rebecca and Ana slipped into their nightclothes and nestled into the feather bed. "I feel like I'm floating in the sky," Rebecca said. "This must be what a tree house is like."

"Exactly like a tree house," Ana laughed, "except for the tree!"

The girls settled into the cool bedding, and Rebecca felt a light breeze riffling the air. Across the street, someone began singing.

In the good old summertime,
In the good old summertime,
Strolling down a shady lane . . .

A wheezy accordion began to play along, and more neighbors joined in the song. Soon the melody drifted from fire escapes and rooftops up and down the street, with a few brave voices harmonizing.

You hold her hand and she holds yours,

And that's a very good sign
That she's your tootsey-wootsey
In the good old summertime.

Rebecca heard the kitchen door opening and heavy footsteps inside. She peered through the open window and saw that Uncle Jacob and Josef had just come home. Rebecca knew from working at Papa's shoe store how tiring it was to work even until suppertime. It was so dark now, it had to be close to nine o'clock. How could her uncle and cousin work such long hours every day? They must feel exhausted.

"Would you like tea?" Aunt Fannie asked softly.

"It's too hot to fire up the samovar," Uncle Jacob said. The icebox door opened. "That lemonade looks wonderful, though."

Glasses clinked in the kitchen. Josef washed at the sink and then pulled a feather bed from under the sofa, where Michael was already asleep. Josef lay down and began to read a book.

"We've got another long day tomorrow," Uncle Jacob told him. "It's good to read, but now you need to sleep."

"I know, Papa," said Josef, "but I've got to keep learning English, or I'll be carrying bundles of coats the rest of my life."

Uncle Jacob sighed. "The heat in the workroom has been unbearable," he told Aunt Fannie. "But Mr. Simon keeps shouting at us to work faster. Ever since the meeting on Sunday, everyone's whispering about going on strike." His voice trailed off as he headed to the bedroom. "I don't know, Fanya. I just don't know . . ."

Aunt Fannie sounded alarmed. "I've heard so much about strikers being attacked on the picket line. Would you be able to watch out for Josef?"

"You know I'd do my best," he promised.

Later, after Josef had finally turned out the light and gone to sleep, Rebecca gave Ana a nudge. "Are you awake?" she whispered.

"Yes," Ana said. "My nightgown is sticking to me like wet paper."

Rebecca unfolded the letter she had been hiding and handed it to her cousin. Ana squinted in the glow from the streetlamps. "Why, it's addressed to the newspaper editor," she said softly. Her eyes widened as she read. "Oh, Rebecca!"

"If people realize how awful it is inside the factory, then surely the city will change the laws," said Rebecca. "That will make the bosses treat the workers fairly, and no one will have to go on strike."

Ana shook her head sadly. "It's a good letter, but there have been dozens of letters in the newspaper already, and nothing ever changes."

Rebecca felt a sinking feeling in her chest. "Maybe if everyone who agreed with us wrote to the newspapers, there might be so many letters that the mayor would see them and realize he has to do something."

"I suppose it's possible," Ana agreed, but she didn't sound convinced. "Michael says the factory owners are more powerful than the mayor, so they do what they want." She patted Rebecca's arm. "But thanks for trying."

Rebecca tucked the letter under her pillow and lay back, looking through the railing onto the street below. Grown-ups sat on the stoops talking and fanning themselves. Young couples strolled along the sidewalks. Lots of them worked at the factories themselves or knew people who did. *What if they all wrote letters,* Rebecca wondered as she closed her eyes.

Tomorrow I am going to mail my letter to the editor. Maybe it will help.

The metallic screech of braking trolleys woke Rebecca with a start. She blinked her eyes open to another hazy morning. The kitchen door creaked shut, and she realized that as late as Uncle Jacob and Josef had come home from work last night, they were already up and leaving again. She rubbed her eyes. The street below was bustling with horse-drawn wagons. Peddlers pushed loaded pushcarts in front of them, heading for their favorite spots. Newsboys shouted out the headlines. "Labor problems at Uptown Coat—read all about it!"

Ana sat up and looked at Rebecca with alarm. "That's where Papa and Josef work," she breathed. Rebecca nodded silently.

The girls scrambled inside through the window, dragging their bedding after them. They stored the feather bed in a corner of the parlor and then helped Michael lay down newspapers on the fire escape. He brought out three unpainted shelves and a fresh can of paint. They watched him brush a shelf with mint-green paint as the newsboys shouted on the street below. The air had cooled slightly overnight, and a sultry breeze was stirring.

"The coat factory workers are about to go on strike, and all I can do is paint shelves," Michael muttered. He kicked at the railing in frustration. "I'm not helping at all." Rebecca knew how Michael felt. There seemed to be so little that anyone could do.

The girls went in to wash and dress. They ate their breakfast rolls in silence at the kitchen table while Aunt Fannie filled the metal work sink with water. She began to scrub clothes against a washboard, making a steady rhythm as lather slid down her arms.

Michael leaned his head in. "How about helping me out?" he called from the fire escape. "I want to get these done this morning, in case it really does rain."

The girls climbed back outside, and Rebecca chose a shelf to paint. She tried to keep her brushstrokes even as the pale green paint glided over the graceful curlicues carved into the smooth wood. *Uncle Jacob is such a good carpenter,* she thought. *He should be building cabinets and furniture all the time, not cutting cloth in a sweatshop.*

The morning slipped by as the three painters bent over their work. After a while, Ana stretched and rubbed her back. "So much bending," she complained. "I need a break—before *I* break!"

"You haven't finished that shelf," Michael said, but he put down his brush and stretched his arms. "I guess I could use a drink of water," he admitted. "Good thing we don't work in a factory!"

"Mrs. Rubin! Mrs. Rubin!" a woman called breathlessly from a nearby window.

Aunt Fannie poked her head out, wiping her wet hands on her apron. "*Nu?*" she asked in Yiddish. "What is it?"

A stream of Yiddish poured from the woman. She was talking so fast, she could hardly catch her breath. "It's the coat factory, Mrs. Rubin! The workers are pouring into the street. They've gone on strike!" Aunt Fannie covered her mouth with her hand.

"Get your hat," yelled the woman. "We're going to march on the picket line."

Aunt Fannie pulled off her apron as the girls scrambled inside.

"Don't go, Mama," Ana pleaded. "There's nothing

you can do. Just wait, and Papa will come home."

Aunt Fannie set her mouth in determination. "Papa and your brother are marching with their fellow workers," she said, "and I will stand beside them."

"I'll come, too," Michael said, leaving his painting. "This can wait."

"No," Aunt Fannie said firmly. "You stay here with the girls. Ana, you and Rebecca will please finish the laundry and hang it up inside." She pinned on a hat, poking in two long hatpins, and took an umbrella from underneath the sink. "A picket line is no place for children."

"What if we stayed right next to you?" Rebecca asked her aunt. "Wouldn't we be safe then?"

Aunt Fannie put her hands on Rebecca's shoulders and looked at her steadily. "The bosses hire men to break up the strike. It gets dangerous." She rushed out the door, calling, "Don't leave here before I get back."

As soon as Aunt Fannie had gone, Michael turned to the girls. "I should be there, too." He pounded his fist against the wall. "I should be doing more to help—much more."

"You're painting shelves to help Papa earn extra

money," Ana said kindly. "It's just as important."

"It's not enough," Michael said bitterly. "Not when Josef has to work so hard. It's not right that I go to school and he can't."

Rebecca felt the letter in her pocket. Maybe Ana was right. Writing to the newspaper wouldn't help enough.

Michael's voice rose. "The more people who protest, the better the chance that the bosses will give in."

That was just what Rebecca had been thinking. "Then we should all go," she said. She had heard Papa talk about other companies that paid better wages and made their factories safer only because the workers had gone on strike. She turned to Ana. "If letters in the paper won't change things, maybe the strike will."

"Mama told us not to leave," Ana argued.

Rebecca knew she shouldn't disobey her aunt, but Michael was right—staying home wouldn't help win the strike. She wondered if Michael would have to work in the factory as soon as the law allowed him to quit school. He was almost fourteen. And what about Ana? Would she have to learn to sew on the noisy machines? The memory of the young stitcher with the pale skin and dull eyes still haunted Rebecca. She couldn't bear the thought of Ana working in such a place.

"If a strike will get people's attention and help change things for the better, then I think we should go," Rebecca said hesitantly. "Papa always says we all have to try to make the world a better place. He and Grandpa tell us *tikkun olam*—'repair the world.' We have to do our part, Ana, even if it might be dangerous."

Michael nodded. His mouth was set in a determined line. Rebecca looked questioningly at Ana, who hung back against the sink full of laundry. The soapy bubbles had burst, and a slick film lay across the dingy water.

"I'm afraid to go," Ana said hoarsely.

"Getting out of Russia was more dangerous than this," Rebecca pointed out. "You have lots of courage, Ana."

Ana shook her head. "Not enough for this."

"Courage comes when you need it," said Rebecca. "I know you want to help your father and your brother. This is our chance!"

The uncertainty faded from Ana's face. She let out a deep breath. "Let's go."

Michael reached for his cap as Rebecca opened the door. She felt a prickle of fear at what she was about to do. Ana, Michael, and Rebecca stepped into the dark hallway, and Ana closed the door behind them. The click of the lock reminded Rebecca that she couldn't turn back.

A Losing Battle

CHAPTER 13

few blocks from the coat factory, Rebecca heard a raucous din, louder than the factory machines and louder than the thunder that rumbled across the sky. As Rebecca, Ana, and Michael drew closer, the noises became more distinct. Feet stomped against cobblestones. Angry voices cut the air like punches. "Strike! Strike!"

The factory building came into view, surrounded by a surging crowd of men and women. Many of the strikers walked with linked arms, while others held signs high above their heads. Rebecca saw signs written in English, Yiddish, Italian, and Russian. "We Shall Fight Until We Win," read one. Another said "In Unity Is Our Strength" in red paint. There was a sense of warm camaraderie, but the strikers looked determined.

Rebecca reached for her cousins' hands. She

scanned the marchers, searching for Ana's family, but the faces blurred together like a movie reel running too fast.

A loud horn blared, and a sleek black motorcar sped up to the curb. Men wearing caps with wide visors pulled low over their eyes jumped out and rushed into the mass of strikers. From under their jackets they pulled short, thick wooden clubs.

"Goons!" Michael shouted above the noise. His hand tightened on Rebecca's. "Stay back!"

The thugs filtered into the crowd. One fell into step behind a striker and suddenly whacked the backs of her knees with his club. The woman fell to the street, crying out in pain. As the thugs tripped and pushed the marchers, some of the women pulled out their hatpins and jabbed the goons. Others used their umbrellas to hit back. Rebecca wondered if that was why Aunt Fannie had used two hatpins and taken her umbrella along.

Within moments, it seemed that everyone was fighting or shoving. Rebecca, Michael, and Ana slowly backed away, watching in horror. Overhead, thunderclouds rolled across the sky, blocking the daylight and turning the street almost as dark as night. Above the tumultuous din, Rebecca heard the clatter of hooves and the clang of bells as horse-drawn wagons raced up the street.

"It's the police!" she shouted with relief. "Now they'll arrest the goons and protect the workers."

Blue-uniformed policemen clambered out of the wagons, blowing their whistles. As Rebecca and her cousins watched in disbelief, the police ignored the thugs and collared the strikers instead.

"What are they doing?" Rebecca cried. "They're hitting the strikers with nightsticks and dragging them away, even if they're hurt!" She remembered Ana telling her that the factory owners had power in the city. Had they gotten the police to help break the strike?

"We've got to find Mama," said Ana. She broke away and nearly disappeared into the crowd before Rebecca and Michael pulled her back.

Just ahead on the street corner, a young woman stepped onto a wooden soapbox and began to address the crowd. Her voice carried above the uproar, and in spite of the melee, people stopped to listen. Rebecca thought she looked familiar. Was she a stitcher at the coat factory? But this girl's eyes weren't dull and lifeless—they gleamed with strength and hope.

"It's Clara Adler," Michael cried, "from the workers' meeting!" Rebecca strained to hear.

"I am one of you," Clara shouted, and the strikers sent up a cheer. "We work hard for our bosses, and all we ask is to be treated fairly in return." Clara's voice was full of passion, and Rebecca felt her heart swelling with admiration.

Clara continued. "Every worker deserves—" In midsentence, two thugs kicked the soapbox from under her. Clara toppled to the cobblestones, and they dragged her away. The crowd surged forward, pulling Rebecca and her cousins along. Rebecca stumbled against a hard object and discovered it was the wooden box that had been Clara's miniature stage. Banging into the crate seemed to knock an idea into Rebecca's head. She stepped onto the soapbox and fumbled in her pocket for her letter. Could her thoughts encourage the strikers?

"Many workers head to the factory every morning before sunrise and work hard into the night to feed their families," Rebecca read in a loud voice. Those closest to her fell silent, and in a moment she was speaking to an attentive audience. "But they aren't paid fairly. The bosses have to make their jobs better—the hours shorter—and the factories safer!" There was a burst of applause. Rebecca was about to continue when she felt a sharp, stabbing pain as a rock struck her head. The letter flew from her hand. Dark spots clouded her sight, and she crumpled to the street.

When Rebecca opened her eyes, she was in an alleyway. Michael's and Ana's frightened faces peered at her, and the commotion of the strike sounded like a distant echo.

"Can you stand up?" Michael asked, trying to help Rebecca from the street. "We'll never find the others now, and we've got to get you home."

Rebecca struggled to her feet. Images swam dizzily before her eyes. Her head throbbed. Blood had splotched her dress. With Michael and Ana supporting her on both sides, she staggered from the alleyway. A bolt of lightning lit the sky and a thunderclap shook the air as a torrent of rain hammered down. The rain splashed against the cobblestones and streamed down gutters. Rebecca turned and glanced at the chaotic scene behind her. Through the dim light and pouring rain, she glimpsed two familiar figures being roughly pushed into a police wagon. It was Uncle Jacob and Josef.

On Thursday, Rebecca felt as if she had awakened from a dream. She gingerly touched the bandage Mama had put on the night before and tried not to wince.

All morning, neighbors and family streamed into the apartment, asking about Uncle Jacob and Josef and fussing over Rebecca's injury. Still feeling dizzy, Rebecca sat on a chair in the parlor. She was glad when Michael and Ana arrived.

"What were you children thinking, going off to a picket line?" Mama scolded.

"We wanted to help," said Michael.

"We didn't think anyone would get hurt," Ana added. She looked as though she was on the verge of crying. Rebecca winked at her and saw a tiny smile of relief.

"I'm glad we were part of the strike," Rebecca said. Her voice filled with conviction. "I really am, Mama!

Just believing that something is wrong isn't enough. I had to do something about it, and this seemed like the right thing."

Rebecca's grandmother threw her hands in the air. "Not only going to picket line, but making a speech, yet!" Bubbie cried. "What if that rock had hit your eye? Stirring up trouble is a dangerous business. When you find hornet's nest, you don't poke it with stick!"

Rebecca was relieved when Mama and Bubbie went back into the kitchen to fix tea. She needed time to think, without everyone scolding her. Maybe they were right—maybe it had been foolish to go to the strike. It certainly had proved to be dangerous. Most of all, Rebecca was sorry that they hadn't accomplished anything by going. Dejected, she scuffed her shoe against the chair leg.

Rebecca felt someone lifting her chin, and she looked up into Lily's pert smile. "How's my favorite kidlet?" Lily asked softly, perching on the arm of the chair. "Don't you worry a bit about that cut ruining your movie face. Even if the scar doesn't fade, your hair will hide it. You're still going to knock 'em dead with those beautiful eyes."

Rebecca flushed. She knew Lily was just kidding to raise her spirits, but the mention of movies reminded Rebecca that going to the strike was not the only thing she had done that was sure to upset her parents and grandparents. That is, if they ever found out about her movie role.

"I guess I shouldn't have gone to the strike," she admitted quietly.

"Says who?" Lily leaned closer and lowered her voice even more. "Listen, doll-baby, you made the world a little bit better by speaking out for what you believe in. Nobody can fault you for wanting to see more fairness in the world. Just remember that the best we can do in this life is follow our hearts."

Rebecca leaned gratefully into Lily's hug. *The best we can do in this life is follow our hearts.* Rebecca knew she had also followed her heart when she acted in the movie. She decided she wouldn't tell her family about that for a long, long time—if ever.

Aunt Fannie paced back and forth, holding a glass of tea absently. "If only Jacob and Josef are not hurt," she fretted.

"And if only Papa and Max have enough money to

bail them out," said Rebecca's brother Victor. "If not, the court will sentence them to the workhouse."

"What about the goons—those men who hurt the strikers and hit me with a rock?" Rebecca asked. "Why aren't *they* in jail?"

"Because the city cares more about keeping the factories running than helping the workers," said Michael with disgust. "The factory owners can get away with anything."

Sadie handed Rebecca a steaming glass. "Don't get excited," she said soothingly. "Drink some tea."

Sophie whispered, "I put in two lumps of sugar."

Footsteps sounded on the stairway, and everyone stared anxiously at the door. Max and Papa came in first, followed by Uncle Jacob and Josef. Aunt Fannie nearly spilled her tea as she ran to embrace her husband and son. They had dark circles under their eyes and angry purple bruises on their faces. Mama settled them comfortably in the parlor, while Aunt Fannie and Bubbie bustled about filling plates of food for them.

"How is the strike going?" asked Michael.

"There is one good result so far," Uncle Jacob answered. "The bosses are going to meet with the strike leaders. The owner of the coat factory has agreed to listen to their complaints and discuss solutions. The workers won't get everything they want, but some things should get better."

Rebecca's spirits lifted. The strike was working! Then she saw Uncle Jacob's shoulders slump. He buried his face in his hands. What was wrong? Even if the workers didn't get everything they wanted, wasn't it still a victory?

When Uncle Jacob looked up, his eyes were filled with despair. "There is one more thing. All the workers who were arrested have been fired. And they will make sure no other factory hires us either. We'll be labeled as troublemakers."

"Then what good did it do for us to strike?" Josef asked angrily. "It doesn't matter what improvements the bosses make—it won't help us!"

Rebecca saw Aunt Fannie's face cloud with disappointment, and tears trickled down Ana's cheeks. Uncle Jacob and Josef losing their jobs was exactly what they all had feared. Had they been wrong to support the strike?

"We had to try to make things better," Uncle Jacob

said. "What else could we do?" He looked at Josef. "Remember, tikkun olam. Maybe the strike won't help you and me, but it will help all workers who come after us." Josef placed his hand on his father's shoulder, and Uncle Jacob pressed his own over it.

Changes in the Air

CHAPTER 14

ooray—today's the picnic at Battery Park!" Benny cried, clapping his hands together. Then he pouted. "But I won't get a haircut." He stamped his foot.

"Haircut?" Rebecca asked. "What makes you think you'd go to the park for a haircut?"

"Mama said there'll be a barbershop at the picnic," Benny answered. "But I don't want a haircut!"

Rebecca and her sisters giggled. "That's a barbershop *quartet,*" Sophie explained patiently. "That means four men who sing songs in harmony. They aren't really barbers!" Benny looked puzzled.

"You'll hear them sing at the picnic," Mama said. "And don't worry, I definitely wouldn't let a singer cut your hair before your very first day of school." She smiled, but Rebecca thought Mama looked a bit wistful, almost as if she was sorry to see Benny start kindergarten.

"Labor Day always seems like the last day of summer to me," Sadie said. "Before you know it, school starts. No more lazy days!"

The weather had changed dramatically after the thunderstorm last week, and the air was refreshingly cool. Something else had changed, too—Uncle Jacob and Josef were out of work. Aunt Fannie talked about taking in a boarder to help pay the rent, but where would a boarder sleep in their cramped tenement?

At the entrance to Battery Park, Ana and her family joined Rebecca's family.

"How are you feeling?" Ana asked Rebecca. "Are you still dizzy?"

"Just a little. I won't be able to run in the three-legged race," Rebecca said. "But I'm lots better."

Ana breathed in deeply. "Don't you love the cool weather? I heard a peddler on Orchard Street say the air is as crisp as a fresh apple." The girls laughed.

The two families spread out their blankets in a spot with a good view of the bandstand. The band members were tuning their instruments, and the many different notes added to the festive commotion all around.

"Come on, Benny, let's go play catch," Victor said, and Rebecca's brothers headed to an open space on the grass.

Rebecca spotted Max and Lily arriving with a group of people she recognized from the moving picture studio. L.B. Diamond, the director who had given her a part in his movie, looked dashing in a sporty coat and high boots. And there was Roddy Fitzgerald, the friendly studio carpenter who had let her crank the phonograph at lunch that day. Rebecca felt rather shy around the director, but she wanted to say hello to Roddy.

The rest of her family was unpacking the picnic lunch. "Mama, I see Max and Lily. I'll go get them," Rebecca said quickly. She got up and hurried toward the group before Mama could tell her to sit still.

"How's the old bean?" Max asked, squinting at her forehead.

"Covered by the beanie," Rebecca quipped, pointing to her hat.

"Doll-baby, it's good to see you looking chipper again," said Lily. She turned to the director. "L.B., you remember my kid sister from *The Suitor,* don't you?"

"Ahh, the kidlet!" said L.B., shaking Rebecca's hand. "Who could forget those great big eyes?"

Rebecca felt herself blushing, pleased that he remembered her. "Hello, Mr. Diamond," she said politely. Then she turned to the carpenter. "Hi, Roddy." It was so good to see the whole crew again!

Roddy doffed his hat and gave a short bow. "Greetings, missy. I hear you had a bit of an adventure at the coat factory last week."

"Yes, I—I did," Rebecca stammered, taken by surprise.

"My wife's sister works at that self-same factory," Roddy went on. "She saw you start to give your speech. She says you're a mighty brave lass."

Rebecca's cheeks felt warm. She hadn't expected anyone outside her family to know about the speech, but she was glad that Roddy approved.

Rebecca led Max and Lily to where the rest of the family had set out their blankets. Lily unpacked her basket and offered Max an array of tempting foods. Max beamed at Lily as each dish was laid out. Victor and Benny had returned and seemed to have worked up quite an appetite after their game. As everyone ate and chatted, the band played rousing patriotic songs that got the crowd clapping in rhythm. Then the musicians gave a drumroll as a stout man stepped to the front of the bandstand and held a megaphone to his mouth.

"That is Mr. Levy from the garment workers' union," Uncle Jacob told them. "He set up the meeting we went to."

"Labor Day became a national holiday twenty-one years ago," Mr. Levy began. His voice resonated across the park. "It was set aside as a day to honor all workers. Yet most factory workers will lose a full day's pay for taking today off for the holiday." The crowd booed.

The speaker lowered the megaphone and held up his hand to silence the audience. "But with every strike, some progress is made," he continued. "When workers and their families stand up for justice in spite of danger, people are forced to take notice. Just last week, a young lady stepped up to address the strikers at the Uptown Coat Company and was shamelessly attacked by thugs hired by the factory owners."

"Clara Adler," Rebecca whispered to Ana and

Michael, and they nodded solemnly, remembering how the young speaker had been knocked from her soapbox and dragged away.

Mr. Levy kept talking. "I'm told that the brave little lady is here today, and we hope she will step forward and deliver the message that she was prevented from reading last week." The crowd clapped with enthusiasm. Rebecca looked around for Clara Adler, delighted that she would finally get to hear her speak. Mr. Levy's voice rang out again. "Will Rebecca Rubin please join me at the bandstand?"

Rebecca's family looked at her in astonishment, but nobody was more surprised than Rebecca. "What shall I do?" she mumbled.

"Your audience awaits you," Max said, helping Rebecca to her feet. "Get up there and wow 'em!"

Rebecca's head felt light, but it was from the surprise of the moment, not her injury. She picked her way through the crowd, and when she stepped onto the bandstand, Mr. Levy pumped her hand up and down and then motioned her to the front.

Rebecca had lost her letter in the melee at the strike, and she didn't know what to say. For a moment she simply stared at the expectant crowd. Gazing out at the upturned faces, Rebecca looked at her own family, gathered together on the grass. Her parents and grandparents, cousin Max, and Ana's family had all come to America for better lives. Now Uncle Jacob and cousin Josef had lost their jobs in the struggle for fair treatment. Rebecca realized she didn't need to read her letter. What she had to say was in her heart.

"When my uncle and cousin came to America," she began, "they got jobs in the coat factory and worked hard twelve hours a day. But the factory was a dark, dirty, dangerous place, and the bosses were very unfair to the workers. So my uncle and cousin joined the strike, hoping to make things better. They were fired from their jobs, but they didn't fail in their efforts. Finally, the bosses will make changes!" People cheered. "Thanks to the strike, the factory will be a better place to work." Rebecca paused, remembering her uncle's words to Josef. "Maybe not for my uncle and cousin, but for all the workers who come after them." Applause erupted through the audience.

Rebecca felt as if another voice had come from her mouth. She hadn't known she could make a speech.

Maybe that was part of being an actor. You could stand in front of an audience without being afraid and give people something to think about, something to remember. Rebecca hoped she had done that today.

"Well, Rebecca," said Papa as she returned to the blanket, "you are a natural in front of a crowd. You're going to make a fine teacher someday." Mama nodded proudly.

"You're a girl with chutzpah," Grandpa exclaimed.

"I always said she was a born actress," Max commented.

Rebecca's head was spinning. If only she had the chutzpah to tell her parents that she wanted to be an actress—not a teacher.

Max cleared his throat. "I hate to move the spotlight, but I have some good news and some bad news to share." Everyone looked at him expectantly. "First the bad news—my movie studio, Banbury Cross, is moving to Hollywood, California."

"Oh, Max," Mama cried. "Have *you* lost your job, too?"

"Not at all," Max reassured her. "In fact, I'm going to be the studio's lead male actor—out in California."

"Is that good news," Mama sighed, "or bad news? I'm not sure which."

"What's so different?" Bubbie asked. "You move from one place to another, but always you come back."

"Not this time," Max said. "Hollywood's going to be my home. All the studios are moving out there. The weather is sunny and warm all year, perfect for shooting outdoors. California has every possible setting—mountains, deserts, forests, and ocean, as well as cities. Mark my words, this is just the beginning of something too big to even imagine. And I'm planning to be part of it."

Grandpa was shaking his head and smiling at the same time. "What do you know? Whoever thought our Moyshe would amount to anything? But this Max—" He slapped Max on the shoulder. "Look at him, a real success. Mazel tov!"

Rebecca was stunned. Max was going to move across the whole country! She might never see him again—certainly not for a long time. Her voice quivered as she asked, "What about Lily?"

"That's the rest of the good news." Max smiled. "Lily's coming to California with me—or I'm going with her!" He took Lily's hand. "We're getting married first, and everyone is invited."

"A wedding!" Sadie and Sophie exclaimed.

"What wonderful news," Mama said. "Oh, Max, I'm so happy for you both."

Lily took a dainty diamond ring from her pocket and slipped it onto her finger. She held out her hand so everyone could admire the sparkling stone. "I hated to take it off, even for an hour," she said, "but I didn't want to spoil the surprise."

So that was the secret Lily had been saving for just the right moment. Rebecca realized she wasn't the only one who had been keeping a secret. But now Max and Lily had shared theirs with the family.

While Max and Lily basked in hugs and congratulations, Rebecca swallowed the lump in her throat. She was thrilled that Lily would be part of the family, but she knew she would miss them terribly. Quietly, she left the blanket before anyone saw the tears filling her eyes.

A warm hand slipped into hers, and Rebecca turned to see Ana walking beside her. "Let's go watch the music players," Ana said, and Rebecca nodded gratefully. The girls ambled up to the bandstand and admired the musicians' bright blue jackets with brass buttons as the band played a spirited march.

"Sounds a good deal better than a phonograph, eh?"

Rebecca looked up in surprise. There was Roddy, standing nearby and puffing contentedly on a pipe. She introduced him to Ana and then asked, "Did you hear the news?" Without waiting for an answer, she blurted out, "Max and Lily are getting married!"

"That's grand! Let's tell the bandleader to announce it and embarrass them as much as we can," said Roddy with a mischievous smile. "By the way, that was a mighty fine speech you made."

"Are you the one who gave Mr. Levy my name?" Rebecca asked, and Roddy winked at her from behind his pipe.

The bandleader was only too happy to announce the engagement. The crowd whistled, the band struck up a playful tune, and the barbershop quartet crooned,

Daisy, Daisy, give me your answer, do.
I'm half-crazy, all for the love of you!
It won't be a stylish marriage
I can't afford a carriage . . .

Looking back, Rebecca could see Max and Lily waltzing together. Their studio friends had wandered over and circled the couple, singing along with the chorus. In spite of her sadness at their leaving, she couldn't help feeling happy for them.

But you'll look sweet
On the seat
Of a bicycle built for two.

"Are you moving to Hollywood, too?" Ana asked Roddy when the song ended.

Roddy shook his head. "It's supposed to be a regular paradise out there, but I won't be going."

"You'll be out of a job," Rebecca said. "What will you do?"

"I've always dreamed of having my own business," Roddy replied. "I want to build things that will last longer than a movie set. I'm starting my own construction company to build an apartment house in Brooklyn."

"Brooklyn!" Ana said. "Isn't that awfully far?"

"Not with the subway," Roddy answered. "People are moving out there as fast as housing can be built. It's a humdinger of an opportunity. My new building is going to have everything, including private bathrooms."

"Imagine having a real china bathtub inside your apartment!" Ana marveled.

"That's the idea." Roddy grinned. "I've got the land, and all I need to do is hire a good crew. I can't do everything myself, you know." He frowned. "I'm having a devil of a time finding a plumber, and good cabinetmakers are as scarce as leprechauns."

Rebecca's heart jumped. "I guess you need someone who can make cupboards and shelving and—"

"—and carved mantelpieces," Ana added, catching Rebecca's eye.

"Indeed I do," Roddy said. "And where am I going to find such a man?"

"Ana and I know a fine cabinetmaker," Rebecca cried. "Come with us!" The girls each took one of Roddy's hands and led him to their family's blanket. "Roddy Fitzgerald, meet Jacob Rubin, your new cabinetmaker."

Uncle Jacob stood up to shake Roddy's hand, looking confused. "What is this all about?" he asked. The two men began to talk about carpentry, and in a few minutes, Roddy offered Uncle Jacob a job.

Uncle Jacob shook Roddy's hand warmly. "This is much more than I was making in coat factory," he said. "My son Josef, he could go to school." Then he hesitated. "This Brooklyn—it is far?"

"Well, it's a bit of a haul from here," Roddy admitted. "I plan to move out there. Maybe you'll want to settle there with your family so that you won't have to travel to get to work. The air is cleaner, and the rents are a good deal lower."

Once again, the family was full of smiles and congratulations as word of the new job spread. This time, Rebecca could share in the joy with everyone else.

The band began playing a lively folk tune, and people got up to dance. They formed a line that grew longer and longer as more people joined in. Soon the line began to snake around the park. Papa took Mama's hand and led her in, followed by Max and Lily and Uncle Jacob and Aunt Fannie. Rebecca's sisters and brothers and cousins linked hands and began to dance. Rebecca couldn't just sit and watch. She joined the line next to Ana and Michael and let the music move her feet.

When the dance ended, Max fell into step beside Rebecca as they walked back to the blanket. "I was awfully proud of you today," he said. "How did you like being on a stage again?"

Rebecca reflected for a moment. "Well, I'm glad I thought of something to say. But it wasn't as much fun as being in a movie."

"No, it's not the same at all," Max agreed. "There's a big difference between acting on a set and *taking* action. And you are certainly a lady of action!"

Rebecca considered the difference. "You once said movies let people forget their troubles," she said at last. "But speeches can help people *solve* their troubles, can't they?"

Max nodded. "People like to get away from their worries for a while, and movies are wonderful for that. But there are times when we need to face problems head-on in order to fix them. That's what speeches can do."

When they reached the blanket again and Rebecca settled back down beside Papa, she knew there was one more speech she had to make. But she couldn't think of a way to start.

The band began playing a slow, lilting melody, and suddenly Rebecca thought of a way. "Papa, my teacher Miss Maloney once told us that America is a great melting pot," she began. "But I think America is more like a band. People play all different instruments, and together they make music." She looked around at her family. They were all listening. "Papa, your music is running the store and helping people who need shoes. Uncle Jacob's is building things out of wood. Bubbie's music is teaching us to cook and sew. As for me—my music is acting." She took a deep breath. "I don't want to be a teacher, Papa. That would be the wrong note for me." Now her words flowed faster. "When I visited Max's studio last spring, I got a part in the movie, and now I'm sure I want to be an actress."

Papa face darkened. "You acted in a moving picture—"

"—and you didn't tell *us*?" Sadie cut in.

"And you didn't invite us to *see* it?" Sophie added.

"You're in for it now," Victor said to Rebecca under his breath.

"Why, I—I—I declare!" Mama sputtered, fanning herself with her hand.

Bubbie shook her finger at Rebecca. "What were you thinking, not to tell your own family? What are we—nobodies?"

"This moving pitcher," Grandpa said sternly, "it's respectable?"

"Of course it is," Lily piped up. "*I'm* in it!"

"She's the star," Max said proudly. "In fact, we met on the set." He put his arm around Rebecca's shoulders. "The director is not easily impressed, but he thought our Rebecca was a natural talent."

Papa opened his mouth, and then clamped it shut without a word. Rebecca squirmed during the long silence until he finally spoke. "My Rebecca, acting in moving pictures? This I have to think about." Then Papa met Rebecca's eyes. "I guess it's true that we all play different instruments," he said slowly. "I have no doubt that whichever one you play, it's going to be heard by a lot of people. But as for this acting . . . well, I'll have to think about that."

Rebecca let out a long sigh. What a strange day it had been, with so many ups and downs. *Strange, but good,* she decided.

The bandleader made an announcement, and Ana

jumped up. "It's time for the three-legged race!" She looked down at Rebecca. "How about if we just go watch?"

Rebecca shook her head. "I don't want to watch the race." Then she laughed and stood up, taking her cousin's hand. "I want to enter it!"

Mama lifted her eyebrows. "You've had a big day already, Rebecca. Are you sure you're up to it?"

Rebecca nodded. Suddenly, she felt she could do just about anything.

INSIDE Rebecca's World

In Rebecca's time, feature films had been around for about ten years and were extremely popular. All movies were silent. Sometimes writing appeared on the screen to explain the action or show what the actors were saying. A pianist played along with the movie, adding the right kind of music to each scene. Girls in 1914 loved watching movies and admired movie stars just as much as they do today.

Many adults thought movie acting was a lower art form than stage acting. Also, actors were often out of work, so most parents did not want their children to become involved in show business. But as the film industry grew, movie actors began to command high salaries. By the time Rebecca would have been a young woman, movie acting was viewed by most people as a respectable way to make a living.

Audiences loved child actors. One girl, Helen Badgley, began acting as a baby, and by 1914 she was a big star, even though she was only five. Two years later, she had to drop out of a movie because she had lost her two front teeth and had to wait until new ones grew in!

The movie industry began in New York and New Jersey, but the studios had already discovered the mild weather of Southern California, where they could shoot outdoors in better light all year round. Within a few years, the studios moved to Hollywood.

Most of today's major film studios—such as MGM, Fox, and Warner Brothers—were started by Jewish immigrants. They were hungry for new opportunities, and they had a hunch that movies would soon be the most popular form of entertainment in America. They were right!

The majority of Jewish immigrants, however, found work in clothing factories, not movies. They worked long, hard hours for little pay. The workers who got the lowest pay and the worst treatment were teenage girls and young women, like the stitchers Rebecca saw. Their mistreatment drove some of them to become leaders in changing the factories.

Clara Lemlich, a young Jewish immigrant, led a strike of 20,000 girls and women that shut down many of New York's shirtwaist factories. For three months, the young women walked the picket line in the winter rain and snow. They were beaten by thugs and arrested by police. But finally, they won shorter hours and higher wages—and inspired other workers to fight for their rights. Years of strikes by all kinds of workers eventually led to the standard 40-hour work week and safer working conditions that Americans enjoy today.

Jewish people have always deeply valued fairness, equality, and opportunity. Like Rebecca, these new Americans were willing to stand up and speak out for what's right.

GLOSSARY

Bar Mitzvah (bar MITS-vah)—the ceremony honoring a boy's first reading of the Hebrew Bible before the congregation, and also the boy himself. Hebrew for "son of the commandment."

bubbie (BUH-bee)—the Yiddish word for *grandmother*

bubeleh (BUH-beh-leh)—the Yiddish way to say *darling* or *sweetie*

chutzpah (HOOTS-pah; first syllable rhymes with "puts")—the Yiddish way of saying *boldness, nerve*

entrez (on-tray)—the French word for *enter*

kosher (KOH-sher)—a Yiddish word meaning *fit to eat* under the Jewish dietary laws

kvetching (KVETCH-ing)—the Yiddish word for *complaining*

mademoiselle (mad-mwah-zel)—French for *young lady*

matzo (MOT-zuh)—the Yiddish word for a large, square cracker eaten instead of bread during Passover. It can also be ground into matzo meal and made into matzo balls for soup, or used instead of flour in baking.

mazel tov (MAH-zl tof)—Hebrew for *congratulations!*

mensch (mench)—in Yiddish, an honorable person

meshugah (meh-SHOO-gah)—*crazy*, in Yiddish and Hebrew

nu (noo)—a Yiddish expression with many meanings, often used like "Well?" or "So tell me!"

oy (oy)—a Yiddish exclamation, similar to "oh!"

oy vey (oy VAY)—a Yiddish exclamation meaning *oh dear!*

seder (SAY-der)—a Hebrew word for the ceremonial dinner

held on the first night or the first and second nights of Passover

Shabbos (SHAH-bis)—Yiddish for *Sabbath*, the day of rest

tikkun olam (tee-KOON oh-LAHM)—in Hebrew, *repair the world*; the Jewish belief that each person should do his or her part to make the world a better place

Torah (TOR-uh)—the first five books of *Jewish Scripture*, usually written on a scroll

Read more of REBECCA'S stories,

available from booksellers and at *americangirl.com*

Classics

Rebecca's classic series, now in two volumes:

Volume 1:

The Sound of Applause

Rebecca uses her talents to help cousin Ana escape Russia. Now she must share everything with Ana—even the stage!

Volume 2:

Lights, Camera, Rebecca!

Rebecca gets the best birthday present ever—a role in a real movie. But she can't tell anyone in her family about it.

Journey in Time

Travel back in time—and spend a day with Rebecca!

The Glow of the Spotlight

Step inside Rebecca's world and the excitement of New York City in 1914! Bargain with street peddlers, and audition for a Broadway show. Choose your own path through this multiple-ending story.

Mysteries

More thrilling adventures with Rebecca!

The Crystal Ball

Will a visit to a fortune teller reveal the truth about Mr. Rossi?

A Bundle of Trouble

Rebecca realizes the baby she's caring for is in danger—and so is she.

Secrets at Camp Nokomis

Rebecca's camp bunkmate seems nice, but what is she hiding?

A Sneak Peek at

The Glow of the Spotlight

My Journey with Rebecca

Meet Rebecca and take an unforgettable journey in a book that lets *you* decide what happens.

The dance audition is finally over, and it was definitely my best performance ever. Still, when my teacher, Ms. Amelia, chose me to do a solo for the winter recital, I was stunned. I never expected her to pick me after what happened last spring: I was onstage with my class, and when I looked out at the audience, I froze. I couldn't dance—or even move. Ms. Amelia actually had to come out and lead me off! I'll never live it down. Even my twin sister, Megan, who rarely misses a chance to embarrass me, felt so bad for me that she was extra nice for weeks. So today I am beyond thrilled that my teacher had enough faith to let me try again.

But as happy as I was, it didn't last long—the day ended up in a terrible fight with my friend Liz. She got totally rattled when she flubbed a few steps of her routine. She managed to finish, but definitely didn't do as well as she could have, and she didn't get a special part in the recital. I tried to make her feel better, but she accused me of thinking I'm a better dancer than she is, which isn't true at all. In fact, the truth is that the thought of dancing by myself on that huge stage makes my stomach churn. But I know that if I ever want to be a pro, I have to get over my stage fright!

Now it's late afternoon, and Mom, Megan, and I are walking down West 39th Street toward the pier to catch the ferry home. Suddenly my mother stops in her tracks. "Oh, look at this gorgeous antique shop," she says. "I've been wanting to stop in here for ages." She peers into the window. "Oh, girls, I see the perfect mirror. We have some time to kill before we catch the ferry. Let's take a look."

Megan and I follow Mom into the shop, rolling our eyes at each other. The mirror is just inside, and I have to admit that it's really rather elegant, with leafy vines carved into its dark wood frame. I can just picture it in her bedroom. Mom walks casually up to the dealer and asks how old it is. The dealer looks kind of like an antique herself. Her hair is pure white, and she's wearing a long skirt and a high-collared blouse with a brooch at the neck.

While Mom and the dealer discuss the price, I stand in front of the mirror, admiring the way the glass can tilt forward or back in its stand. I'm in my favorite school outfit, and I twirl in front of my reflection. The shimmery purple fabric of my skirt fans out, and the sequined flowers on the front sparkle.

I can't resist doing a bit of my dance routine while I look in the mirror. Megan groans as if I'm totally embarrassing her. As usual, she's wearing jeans and a baggy sweatshirt that says *Harvard*. As if she's going there anytime soon. I mean, we're only ten!

Megan and I are twins, but we don't look alike or do the same things. She loves museums, I love theater. She wants to be a doctor, like our dad, while I want to be a dancer. We don't even like the same books or video games. Sometimes I wish we were better friends, but most of the time it feels as if she and I are just plain opposites.

Like right now: she plops herself down in an overstuffed armchair and pulls out her science book.

"I see Megan is getting a start on her homework," Mom says to me. "I might need a few minutes to decide about this mirror, so why don't you study your times tables. Didn't you say there's a quiz tomorrow?"

"Mo-o-om . . . " I protest, but she waves me off. She's already bargaining with the antique dealer, trying to get the woman to drop her asking price. She points

out a few chips in the glass.

The dealer considers this, and then shakes her head.

"How about free delivery?" my mother presses.

This is going to take a while. Sighing, I plop down in a creaking leather chair and drag my dance bag closer.

Inside, next to my arithmetic workbook, are my tap shoes and the tuxedo costume. I open my book to the first page of times tables and try to concentrate on that instead of thinking about my fight with Liz.

I don't really know how the argument got started. I was trying to make Liz feel better, but she accused me of only caring because I knew I had a solo. It isn't true! I was so hurt that I lashed out and told her she was just jealous. As soon as I said it, I felt a terrible hole in my chest. I apologized right away, but Liz threw her tap shoes into her bag and stormed out of the dressing room.

I don't want to lose a good friend over a dance recital, but I just don't know what to do now.

The store is so quiet I can hear the clock ticking, and it's hard to concentrate. Unlike Megan, who's a whiz at math, I've never been very good at it. Why do I need to memorize the times tables when I'm going to be a famous dancer?

I try again. "Mom, we're going to miss the ferry." We live in New Jersey, which is across the Hudson River from New York. We ride the ferry into the city every week for my dance classes.

Mom gives me a sympathetic smile. "It'll just be a few more minutes, honey. We've got plenty of time." She hands Megan her phone. "Give your father a call and let him know we'll be home in time to make dinner."

I close the workbook and rummage through my purse, finding two quarters and a crumpled dollar bill. Maybe there's something interesting here that doesn't cost too much. I wander over to a table filled with old-fashioned toy cars, metal mechanical banks, and china dolls. Suddenly I spot a painted wooden doll. It has a flat bottom and stands there looking at me sweetly. Swirly designs with leaves and flowers surround a smiling face. Painted hands are folded across a flowery dress. As I reach for it, the dealer says, "That's an old Russian nesting doll." I guess I look clueless, because she explains, "If you pull the top and bottom apart, there are smaller dolls nesting inside."

I tug the two halves, and sure enough, a smaller doll appears inside. Cute! On I go, opening each doll to reveal a smaller one. The last one is so tiny I can't imagine how the artist painted it so perfectly. I line up the dolls on the table, falling in love with each one. I turn over the largest doll, looking for a price tag.

The dealer studies me with a curious expression. "I played with those often as a girl. I'm rather attached to them," she says. "Do put the set back together when you're done, won't you?" She turns back to my mother.

I don't see a price tag, but if the set is special to her, I suppose it must be expensive. I sit down on the floor and begin putting the dolls back together. I place the tiniest one inside the next smallest doll, carefully lining up the painted hands, when the room starts to spin. I steady myself against the table, thinking the audition must have really worn me out. Then everything around me is lost in a blur.

A cool breeze washes over me and I blink. Instead of a table of antique toys beside me, I'm sitting against a low brick wall at the edge of a flat rooftop. My heart starts pounding. What happened to the antique store, and Mom, and Megan—and *where on earth am I?* Standing up, I peer over the edge of the wall to the street below. It's lined with a row of tidy three-story apartment houses that have high front steps. At least I'm still in Manhattan—I think. But instead of honking taxis and cars, the street is clogged with people and horse-drawn wagons. A horn sounds: *Ah-oo-ga! Ah-ooh-ga!* I shake my head and blink, but when I look again, a shiny black antique car comes chugging and sputtering up the street. Is this a parade?

Behind me, a soothing voice says, "There you go, Gray-Wing." Turning around, I see a girl about my age with long copper-brown hair, feeding a pigeon in a cage. In fact, there's a whole row of pigeon cages against the far wall, and I hear a chorus of coos. Could this be a dream?

Suddenly, the girl begins to sing in a beautiful clear voice. I duck behind a stack of wooden crates and watch her. She's wearing old-fashioned high button boots and a dress with violet stripes. Her hair is tied back with a big purple velvet ribbon.

I guess she likes purple as much as I do.

If this is a dream, it sure feels real. Should I try to talk to the girl?

She's singing to the pigeons as if they're her audience, but she's nothing like some of the show-offs at the dance studio. I start to stand, but then think better of it. It's all just too strange!

I glance down and realize that I'm still holding the two smallest Russian dolls, one nestled inside the other. Suddenly I flash back to my last moment in the antique store, when I put the dolls together. Did the dolls somehow, magically . . . ? It doesn't make any sense, but then dreams often don't. My fingers trembling, I separate the larger doll, so that the smallest one peeks out. Then I fit the larger doll back together, lining up the design of the hands—and once again everything around me spins into a blur and disappears.

Almost instantly, the dizziness passes and I'm back inside the antique shop.

Disoriented, I step away from the table and stumble into a small wooden wagon filled with dolls.

There's a huge clatter as the dolls fall and knock each other over like dominoes. Mom gives me a sharp look.

"Nothing's broken!" I call, feeling shaky.

Megan slams her book closed. "Can't you stay still for one minute? I'm trying to read my science book. Did you already finish studying for your multiplication quiz?" But Megan really isn't asking, because she knows the answer is no.

I stare down at the dolls in my hand. I don't know if I fell into a dream or a hidden time warp, but whatever it was, I want go back. If I can get there again, this time I'll talk to that girl who was singing and feeding the pigeons. Maybe we could become friends. And since no time passes here while I'm in that other world, Mom won't even notice that I'm gone. She's still haggling with the dealer over the price of the mirror, but we'll have to leave soon to catch the ferry. This is my only chance to go back and meet that girl. And if I go, I won't have to deal with Megan, or Liz, or times tables!

Once again, I pull the bigger doll apart, and then push it together neatly, aligning the pattern. In a flash, the room spins, and when I open my eyes and steady myself, I'm back on the same rooftop with the girl in the purple dress. I take a small step forward and clear my throat. I try not to startle her, but she jumps when she hears me. "Sorry," I apologize, and then wonder what to say next.

Before I can come up with an explanation of how I got there, the girl smiles.

"You must be Daisy!" she exclaims. I have no idea who Daisy is, but I have no time to tell her who I really am before she rattles on. "Cousin Max told Papa you might be coming to stay with us for a few days. It must be so exciting to be on the vaudeville circuit."

Did she say *vaudeville*? The theme of the winter recital (when I'll be dancing a solo!) is based on old vaudeville shows. We'll be dancing to songs that were popular a hundred years ago. My tap class is doing a dance that Ms. Amelia says was a big hit back then. Of course, this girl couldn't possibly know about that. But she seems to think vaudeville is cool, so maybe I should tell her!

She stares at my skirt, her eyes practically popping out, as if she's never seen anything like it. Although the sun is setting and the light is fading fast, the sequins still shine. I suppose it looks like a vaudeville costume to her. Her purple dress comes down to her knees and now that she's turned my way, I can see that an apron is covering the entire front of it. Wherever I am, I'm definitely not wearing the right clothes.

I try to speak, but nothing comes out. My sister would never believe that I'm actually speechless!

"You must really miss your parents right now," the girl continues, "but Max told us they'll arrive in a few days. I hope you'll like staying with us. By the way, I'm Rebecca. Did Max tell you that I want to be a performer, too?"

I still don't know where I am or how I got here, but just then, a door opens onto the roof and an older man steps out. He's wearing a loose white shirt and baggy pants with suspenders, and holding two small pails.

Rebecca leans close and whispers, "Uh-oh. It's Mr. Rossi, the janitor. He's grumpy and doesn't like kids."

About the Author

JACQUELINE DEMBAR GREENE used to read historical novels under an apple tree in her yard when she was a girl. She loved to imagine living in a more exciting time and place. While writing about Rebecca, Ms. Greene talked with friends and relatives who recalled their experiences growing up in the early 1900s. She also explored New York's Lower East Side and visited the neighborhoods that would have been part of Rebecca's world. Ms. Greene lives in Massachusetts with her husband. When she isn't writing, she enjoys hiking, gardening, and traveling to visit her two grown sons.